flower

flower

IRENE N. WATTS

Tundra Books

Published in Canada by Tundra Books,
75 Sherbourne Street, Toronto, Ontario M5A 2P9

Published in the United States by Tundra Books of Northern New York,
P.O. Box 1030, Plattsburgh, New York 12901

Library of Congress Control Number: 2004110125

Library and Archives Canada Cataloguing in Publication

Watts, Irene N., 1931–
    Flower / Irene N. Watts.

ISBN 978-0-88776-710-4

    1. Home children (Canadian immigrants) – Nova Scotia – Juvenile
fiction.   2. World War, 1914-1918 – Juvenile fiction.   I. Title.

PS8595.A873F59 2005   JC813'.54   C2004-904121-5

We acknowledge the financial support of the Government of Canada
through the Book Publishing Industry Development Program (BPIDP)
and that of the Government of Ontario through the Ontario Media
Development Corporation's Ontario Book Initiative. We further
acknowledge the support of the Canada Council for the Arts and the
Ontario Arts Council for our publishing program.

Design: Terri Nimmo

Printed and bound in Canada

ONTARIO ARTS COUNCIL
CONSEIL DES ARTS DE L'ONTARIO

This book is printed on acid-free paper that is
100% recycled, ancient-forest friendly (40% post-consumer recycled).

2 3 4 5 6   11 10 09 08 07

For Vicki Duncan

Acknowledgments

As always, thanks to my editors, Kathy Lowinger and Sue Tate.

The following people and institutions have been enormously helpful in the creation of this narrative:

Cathi Zbarsky, Firehall Library, Vancouver, British Columbia

Georgia Robinson, Lindsay Public Library, Lindsay, Ontario

Lorne Gray, Blacksmith, Vancouver, British Columbia

Marlis Lindsay, King Bethune House, Peterborough, Ontario

The Peterborough Centennial Archives

Professor Tania Watts, Department of Immunology, University of Toronto

A lily of a day
Is fairer far in May,
Although it fall and die that night;
It was the plant and flower of light.
In small proportions we just beauties see;
And in short measures, life may perfect be.

From *A Part of an Ode*
Ben Jonson 1572–1637

Contents

TORONTO, ONTARIO, CANADA

June 2005

Katie

I used to talk a lot to my mother. I'd curl up beside her on the couch after school, and tell her about my day. How Miss Jones said Angie and me were chatterboxes, and about the bad boys in my grade one class. I saved up knock-knock jokes and she always laughed, even when I got them mixed up. Dad called us his laughing girls.

One afternoon she said, "Time to teach you how to make Dad's favorite cookies for Christmas."

"Gingerbread," I said.

Mom got the things we needed and handed them to me. I lined them up on the kitchen table one by one, and repeated the names so I'd remember them next time. She showed me how to measure half a cup of brown sugar and three cups of flour, a teaspoon of ginger and a pinch of salt, then two-thirds of a cup of molasses. I broke an egg into a bowl and beat it up with a fork (that was before I hated eggs). We took turns creaming the butter, then Mom added the other ingredients and I poured in the molasses a little at a time. When the mixture was ready, I rolled it out with the big rolling pin and made crescent-moon shapes and stars and trees with my own cookie cutters.

Dad tasted the gingerbread and told Mom it was the best gingerbread she'd ever made. I shouted, "Mom didn't make it, it was me!" Gingerbread became my signature dish, something I always made for Christmas and birthdays.

That year Mom enrolled me in drama classes. I went every Saturday morning and, as soon as I got home, I'd tell her about the stories we'd heard and acted out.

She said, "I love stories."

"Me, too," I said, "and for Halloween I'm going to be a princess, or a witch, or maybe a ghost." I made scary noises and Mom pretended to be frightened. I asked her when she was going to start making my costume, and she said, "There's lots of time before then, Katie." But there wasn't enough time – there was hardly any time left.

Mom died of cancer a few weeks after Christmas, soon after my seventh birthday.

For a long while, I went on talking to her. I'd sit at the dining room table and look up at her picture. Dad told me it was painted when they went on holiday to Greece, the year before I was born.

Mom's eyes are green, not brown like Dad's. In the picture she's smiling at something a long way off. Dad says she's looking at the ocean, but I know she's smiling at me. Her short reddish brown hair is ruffled by the wind and she's tucked her pink shirt into a blue denim skirt.

I thought she was still there inside the picture, that she could hear me when I spoke to her. I told her all kinds of stuff: how I was having problems in school telling left from right, how I mixed up *b* and *d*, how my threes faced the wrong way.

Soon after that, Dad came into my room for a goodnight hug and said, "A kiss for your left hand — the one with the freckle on it — and one for your right. Now go to sleep, Miss Kaitlin Carr. Dad has a mountain of work to finish."

That was how I learned left from right, so I *knew* Mom was still listening to me. I imagined her as a gentle ghost who could put things right. I was a pretty weird kid.

I haven't talked out loud to Mom for years. After she died, Gran (Dad's mother) came to look after us for a while and, when she went back to Halifax, Dad and I muddled on. Actually, we managed pretty well with help from neighbors, invitations to meals, and a lot of take-out dinners from Greek restaurants nearby.

I'm glad we didn't move from the house Mom and Dad bought when they got married. They chose it because it was close to the University of Toronto, where

Dad still works, and because Chester Avenue is right round the corner from Danforth Avenue, which is the center of the Greek district.

My father's an associate professor of biology at the university. He often works late, and sometimes he goes away to give lectures on his research project: "Lymphocyte Development in Chicken Embryos." When I went to meet him one Saturday, he showed me the warming chamber, which held a rack of eggs. He shone a light on the eggs and I saw the embryos inside. They were honestly the most disgusting things I'd ever seen – totally, absolutely, gross. I didn't know how he could face eating eggs ever again. It doesn't seem to bother him. I guess scientists aren't as squeamish as other people. I can't look at an egg without seeing those poor little squirming creatures. I'm even into baking eggless cakes now.

Last year, we redecorated and had the dining room painted terra-cotta. When it was time to put the pictures back, Dad asked me if I'd like to keep Mom's portrait in my room. I hung it on the wall facing my bed. I look up at her sometimes when I'm learning lines for a play, or writing in my journal. She's been dead over six years now, and I guess, most of the time, I've kind of adjusted to losing her.

Actually, I thought about Mom today. We had drama this afternoon, just about the only subject capable of keeping anyone's attention on the last Friday of school before summer vacation. Mr. Keith, our drama teacher, let us do the first read through of *The Secret Garden*. We sat around and took turns reading different parts. When Mary Lennox wakes up in her big house in India, not knowing that everyone has died of cholera, and she's all alone, it reminded me of how quiet our house is, without my happy mother.

There are great roles for all of us: hunchbacked Uncle Archibald; Martha, the maid; Lily, the ghost of Mary's aunt and mother of the spoilt, bedridden boy, Colin, who becomes Mary's friend. Mel really wants to play Dickon, the boy who talks to animals. A lot of the guys do. I wouldn't want to be in Mr. Keith's shoes at audition time. That usually happens the first week we get back to school. I'm desperate to play Mary and can't wait to begin rehearsals.

Angie said, "Don't obsess, Katie. Thank goodness that's months away." I can't help it — what else is there to look forward to? Mel's going on a fishing trip with his dad and Angie is off to an arts camp on Lake Ontario.

After Mom died, I thought we'd always keep the house the way it was. That's not what happened. Things started to change around the time Dad promised to come to the annual fund-raising evening at school. He was late as usual, and snuck in just as the school orchestra finished their first number. Truthfully, he didn't miss much. Our class put on a play with music called *We Shall Never Die*. It's the true story of a mining disaster that happened in an English colliery in 1832. Twenty-six children, aged seven to seventeen, were lost. I was one of the trappers, a young girl who's afraid of the dark. A flood swept through the underground tunnels and the kids whose job it was to open and close the doors as part of the ventilation system drowned.

Dad wanted to know why we couldn't put on something more cheerful, but said he'd make it somehow. If I'd known what was going to happen, I would have moved Heaven and Earth to keep him away. Not because it didn't go well; it did. Some of the parents were even wiping their eyes by the end of the performance, and a huge amount of money was raised for new computers and library books.

When the play was over, the principal went round greeting people. She'd invited her niece – you'd never guess that they were related. Our principal looks like . . . well . . . like a principal. Her niece is tall, with shining blonde chin-length hair. As far as Angie and I could tell, she wasn't wearing any makeup.

"Bet she's a model," Angie mouthed to me. I saw perfect skin, big gray eyes, and one of those skinny bodies that look great in anything. She was wearing black leather pants, a red blazer, and a white silk shirt.

The principal introduced her to Dad. Stephanie told us that she and her brother had recently opened a boutique, Stephanie and Giles, in the Distillery District – a trendy part of downtown Toronto that used to be an old Victorian industrial area. It's being restored into a cool place with coffee bars, boutiques, art galleries, and work spaces.

She congratulated me on my performance, gave Dad her card, and said, "Why don't you bring your daughter to my shop? We've got some lovely things in right now, and it's fun down there."

Nice try, I thought. *Shopping is not the way to my dad's heart.*

"We might do that. Katie's always complaining she's got nothing to wear. Perhaps next Saturday?" Dad said, leaving me speechless.

It got worse, much worse, because five months later they were married.

Dad helpfully pointed out how nice it would be for me to have someone around the house who was only twenty-eight, young enough to be my sister. Is that how he wanted me to think of her, as a sister? I needed a sister about as much as I needed a stepmother.

I thought Dad and I were just fine before she arrived. Dad said, "Nothing is going to change between us, Katie." *Ha-ha, big joke.* Everything has changed, and all the stories I've ever heard or read about stepmothers are coming true.

Step works long hours, so Dad and I more or less continue our routine: we shop and take turns cooking, but I hardly ever have any real time with him. We're not a family anymore. There are the two of them and there's me, and I'm the one who's supposed to adapt.

The day after tomorrow, they're shipping me off to Halifax for three weeks to stay with my grandparents. It was all arranged when Gran and Grandfather came down for the wedding. They've just retired and are converting an old Victorian house into a bed-and-breakfast. I was actually looking forward to going until a couple of weeks ago, when Dad casually announced that he'd been invited to give a talk at a science conference in London. He must have told Stephanie before he told me because she immediately said that Giles would be thrilled to get rid of her *(I bet)* while she's away.

"Dad, that's fantastic," I said. "I'll check the Net and see what plays are on in London." Not that I was thrilled at having to share the trip with Step, but with luck she'd be shopping full-time, so maybe Dad and I would get a chance to do some stuff on our own. "How long are we staying? How much time will we have to go sightseeing after the conference? Can we visit the Yorkshire Moors? Wait till I tell Angie I'm actually going to the place where *The Secret Garden* happens."

"Katie, I'm afraid you're not coming with us this time," Dad said.

My hands went icy cold. I couldn't bear to look at Step. She must have known all along that I wasn't going. I bet she begged Dad to leave me at home. At that moment I didn't just not like her much, I hated her.

"What do you mean, I'm not going, Dad?"

Step mumbled something about making more coffee and headed for the kitchen.

"You promised to visit your grandparents and they're looking forward to seeing you, Katie. It wouldn't be right to disappoint them. This is a working holiday, lots of chicken talk. You'd be bored," Dad said.

"That's the most pathetic excuse I've ever heard. Why can't you at least be honest and say you don't want me tagging along? Dad, I won't get in the way, I promise. I can go places on my own."

"Sorry, Katie, not this time. Stephanie needs a change and so do I. It's only for three weeks. We'll be back by the time you come home."

"It doesn't feel like home to me anymore. You don't care what happens to me. How can you be so mean? Three weeks in England and you're going without me and taking her?"

"Stop the dramatics, Kaitlin. The world cannot revolve around what *you* want all the time. You'll have other opportunities to travel."

"Right, I'm holding my breath."

"I don't want to hear another word about this. Go to your room."

I stormed out, slamming the door as hard as I could.

Next day Stephanie brought me home a pair of designer jeans. Typical – it just showed how brainless, how insensitive she is. A pair of jeans was supposed to make me feel better?

"No, thank you. Do you really think this makes up for leaving me behind?" I said icily, and didn't give her a chance to reply. We all kept out of each other's way for the next few days.

On the second to last night before we go away on holiday, traditionally Dad and I go through the fridge, looking for leftovers. Any food that isn't green with mold or actually walking comes under the knife. Ancient carrots, dried-up mushrooms, onions, whatever we can find is stir-fried. I pour the result over brown rice and somehow it always tastes great. Then, on the last night, when we're all packed, we eat out.

When I walked into the kitchen after school today, Dad was already busy grating a lump of old cheddar cheese. He smiled at me as though nothing had happened. I stood beside him and began to chop tomatoes and onions. He'd even got the rice started.

Step came in and put a box down. I opened it. *Ugh, chocolate cheesecake, disgusting.*

Dad said, "Hello, darling, supper's almost ready." He gave me a look, warning me not to say anything about dessert.

We'd just finished the last of the risotto when Dad said, "We have something to tell you." I thought he was going to surprise me – say it was all a joke and that they were going to take me to England after all. But when I glanced across the table, Step was looking at Dad, and he was looking at her. They'd forgotten all about me and my stomach was in knots, waiting for Dad to speak.

"Can't you guess, Kate?" Step said.

I felt like saying, "I hate guessing games," but instead I looked at Dad and said, "Guess what?"

"We're going to have a baby, around the middle of December." Dad beamed and held Step's hand. "We've been waiting to tell you, Katie. We thought tonight was a good time."

No, Dad, this was not a good time to tell me, in fact, it was a lousy time. Instead I forced myself to congratulate them. "Who wants some of Stephanie's delicious cake?" I inquired sweetly, and started to clear the table, wishing I had enough guts to accidentally drop the cake on Step's lap.

My birthday's on December 17th. I'll be fourteen, practically old enough to be the kid's mother. *I hope no one's expecting me to get up in the night to look after it.*

Step offered to help clean up, but I said, "Don't bother, I'll do it." That's all I needed at that moment, sweet baby talk in the kitchen.

"I think I'll go up to bed, then. I'm tired. Thanks for supper, Kate." She kissed Dad's cheek and went upstairs.

I headed into the kitchen to load the dishwasher. Dad followed me and put his hand on my shoulder. I shrugged it away, and turned to look at him. "Another mouth to feed, Dad?" It was meant to be funny. I guess it turned out sounding the way I really felt, which was pretty upset.

"Katie, can't you be happy about this, make room for the baby? There is room for all of us, you know."

"You forgot *me*, Dad. There doesn't seem to be much room for *me* lately. Oh, and by the way, Angie asked me over tomorrow night, so I won't be going out for dinner with you and Step. Good night." Dad knew I was lying, but I didn't care.

A little while later I heard him come upstairs. I turned off the light and pretended to be asleep. He knocked on my door. I didn't answer. He came in anyway, tucked the duvet round my shoulders, and stood quietly for a minute. Then he left, closing the door behind him.

I felt too miserable to even open my journal. I stared up at Mom's picture and wished I still believed she was there, making everything alright again.

LONDON, ENGLAND

September 1902

Lillie

My mother's name is Helen. She lives in, and I live out.

I've been boarded in ever so many places since I was a baby. I'm six, getting on for seven. At Mrs. Riley's, where I am now, I hem hankies. All day I sit and hem. She slaps me when the stitches are crooked or too big, then I have to do them over. Mrs. Riley says I sew with the wrong hand. She won't let me use my left hand, my *bad* hand she calls it, but that's the only way I can hem. I don't like sewing. Mrs. Riley watches me and hits my knuckles with the wooden spoon if she catches me using my *bad* hand.

When Queen Victoria died last year, we were sewing black armbands all day long. Even the twins, Ethel and Esther, and they're younger than me, were helping.

Rosie's got poor eyes; she can hardly see. Mrs. Riley hates her more than any of us. She gets money paid regular for Rosie – that's why she keeps her.

Mrs. Riley likes her own boy, Bert. He's big and mean, always pinching us. I told Helen he looks up our dresses, and she sighed and said, "Keep out of his way."

The girls sleep together in the bed upstairs. The twins wet the bed, and Mrs. Riley gives them a whipping most days, but not too hard. At the place I was in before this, at Mrs. Tompkins', there were seven children. We slept on the floor after she sold the mattress for drink. Helen took me away from there quick as a wink when she found out. "Don't you ever touch a drop, Lillie, you hear me? Drink gets you in trouble."

I try to remember everything Helen tells me. I think over the words after she's gone back to that big house, where she works for the lords and ladies, and I whisper them to Rosie when the others are asleep. That way I don't forget.

Helen told me we have to pretend we're sisters. I'm not to tell anyone she's my mother, but I *know* she is, it's just that I have to keep it a secret. "I was sixteen when I had you," she said. "If Madam knew I got a little girl and no husband, I'd lose my place."

Helen comes to see me every other Sunday afternoon, and sometimes on Wednesdays. Then she pays Mrs. Riley, who always counts the money Helen gives her before putting it in the teapot on the mantelpiece. Sometimes Helen can't come because she has too much work at the house. She says I mustn't mind, so I try not to. No one ever comes to see Rosie.

Helen and I do special things. Once she took me for a ride on a horse-drawn bus. After we stepped down, the street sweeper winked at Helen, and she tossed her head so that the feather on her hat wobbled. I laughed out loud. Helen pushed her hat pin more firmly into her hair – her hair's golden brown, not black like mine. Mrs. Riley calls me a little Gypsy because my hair's so dark. Helen's ever so pretty. "Cheeky blighter, we can do better than the likes of him, eh, Lillie?" she said.

The house where Helen works is very grand. The dining table seats twenty-four, she told me. She sleeps at the top of the house with Gertie, who helps Nanny with Miss Sadie and Master Rupert and the new baby that lies in a cradle covered with muslin and ribbon and lace. Helen said once, "See, Lillie, I'm not always going to be the maid of all work, filling coal scuttles and polishing grates. One day I'll be a lady's maid, bring Madam her breakfast and arrange her hair, lay out her gown and help her dress when she goes to the opera at Covent Garden. You've got to aim for something in life, Lillie."

She looked at me then, really looked, and said, "Is that Mrs. Riley treating you fair? Feeds you alright, does she?" It wouldn't do to tell Helen I'm hungry all the time, that Bert snatches the bread off our plates. If I get moved again, it could be worse. Best to say nothing about it.

One Wednesday Helen comes and says, "Today's your birthday, Lillie. You're seven years old, so I've brought you a present. It's a picture postcard. Do you like it? That's the famous Lillie Langtry. She's the most beautiful lady in London . . . well, after Queen Alexandra, that is. She's a great friend of King Edward, the one who used to be Prince Bertie. Lillie always wears black, to show off her beautiful white skin. Doesn't she have lovely hair and eyes? You've got nice brown eyes too, Lillie."

In the afternoon we cross the Albert Bridge and look down at the River Thames. Helen says, "Ooh, I would like to go on one of those big ships across the ocean." Helen's always wishing for things. It makes me shiver to look down into that dark water.

We walk along the embankment. My feet hurt, but Helen likes to show me the fine ladies and gentlemen, and the smart carriages driving along. "Can we sit down for a bit, Helen? I'm tired," I say.

"Try thinking about something nice and you'll soon forget you're tired. . . . Well, look who's here, that's a surprise. I didn't expect to see him."

Helen straightens her hat and smiles up at a young man, who whips off his cap and smiles back at her.

"Good afternoon, Miss Helen, this is a pleasure. And who might this be?" he asks, looking down at me.

Helen squeezes my fingers hard. There is no need to do that – I know when to keep quiet.

"Good afternoon, Mr. Charles. My little sister and I are taking a walk; it's her birthday. Say hello to the gentleman, Lillie. He's the under footman where I work."

"Hello," I whisper.

"Doesn't look much like you, does she?" He smiles again at Helen, and her cheeks go pink.

"Her father, my mother's second husband, was a sailor from Malta. She takes after him. She's his spitting image, with all those dark curls. He's dead now."

This is the first time Helen has mentioned my father. I look at her. *Is it true, or is she telling a fib?*

"Come on, Lillie, I've got to get you home," Helen says. But she's standing here looking up at Mr. Charlie, in no hurry to leave as far as I can tell.

"Allow me to escort you to the tea stall across the road, young ladies. And won't you give me the pleasure of buying you a nice cup of tea and a meat pie for little Miss Lillie here?"

The pie is full of meat and onions, with pastry so flaky it melts in my mouth.

"You're late. Supper's over," Mrs. Riley says, when I get back. Bert sticks his tongue out at me, but tonight I don't care that he ate my portion.

A few weeks go by before I see Helen again. There must've been goings-on at the big house. Mrs. Riley is extra mean 'cause the money is late. When Helen does come, Mrs. Riley says, "Ain't forgotten us, then?" She counts the coppers as usual, and Helen says, "It's all there, and a bit over for being late. I'm sorry – I've been poorly with a cough."

Later, when we go out, she gives me a pair of boots wrapped in newspaper. "Miss Sadie outgrew them, and Gertie was supposed to throw them out. I'd told her about you and how fast you're growing. I can trust her; she's my friend. She asked me to get rid of them, and winked when she handed them over."

I've never had anything so beautiful to wear before. The leather is soft and the boots are only a little bit too big. We stuff newspaper in the toes. Then I wrap the boots up again and hide them under my shawl. Later I put them under the bed, in the corner. I do the sweeping so Mrs. Riley won't see them, unless she's snooping.

This afternoon Helen said, "You remember that nice Mr. Charles? Last week he took me to the Music Hall. We sat up high in the gallery and looked down at all the toffs and their ladies, and the commotion in the private gold boxes – the ladies fanning themselves and drinking champagne. Lovely it was. There was this singer, Lottie Collins. She's been to America and is ever so famous. She came out on the platform, with all the lights shining round her. She was wearing the most beautiful red satin dress. When she danced, she lifted up her skirt and showed her petticoats. Rows and rows of frills, hundreds there must've been. She sang a song, and got us all to sing the chorus: 'Ta-ra-ra Boom-de-ay, Ta-ra-ra Boom-de-ay.' " Helen sang it for me and I hummed along.

"On the way home, Mr. Charles bought me a bunch of violets from a flower-seller. First time anyone bought me flowers. I felt like a real lady. This one's for you. I pressed one of the violets under the washstand."

"Oh, Mother . . . I mean Helen, thank you."

"We share, don't we? You're my little girl. I'll take care of you, don't you worry."

"Where are we going now, Helen?" I said.

"I'm going to show you a place, and I want you to remember the way, so you can find it by yourself if ever you need to. Stepney Causeway, it's called." She made me say it out loud three times, so I wouldn't forget. We sang it to the tune of "Ta-ra-ra Boom-de-ay." Then we stopped in front of this big gray building.

"Looks dark, Helen. I don't like it. It makes my stomach feel funny."

All her good mood gone, she said sharply, "You stop that kind of talk, Lillie. It's a big place, that's all. As big as Buckingham Palace, where the king and queen live. It's a fine place. There are some words written over the door. I'll read them to you, and don't you forget what they say: NO DESTITUTE CHILD EVER REFUSED ADMISSION. That means, it's for boys and girls who have no place else to go. You can knock at the door, and they'll take you in and feed you and look after you." Then she grabbed my hand and we turned around to go back to Mrs. Riley's.

"Cheer up, my little Lil," Helen said, and started to sing again. I joined in. A window opened above us and a man threw us a penny. We laughed so hard Helen began to cough, and then couldn't stop. She put her handkerchief to her mouth and, when she took it away, I saw a drop of blood.

When we got back to Mrs. Riley's, she patted my cheek and said, "Be a good girl." Then she walked off into the rain and I could hear her coughing all the way down the alley.

I wait and wait for her for three Sundays and a Wednesday. I lose count how many weeks she doesn't come. Mrs. Riley gets crosser and crosser, and slaps me more often. Some days I go without supper.

One morning she tells Bert to get his jacket. "We're

going uptown to see what's what. Lillie, finish them pile of hankies, if you know what's good for you."

They are gone a long time. None of us has anything to eat at midday. I am hemming the last of the hankies when they come back. Mrs. Riley sends the others upstairs.

"I got something to tell you, Lil. It's bad news. Helen's gone. Died and gone to Heaven. The cough killed her. Tuberculosis, her friend Gertie said. Them people she works for paid for the funeral."

I look down at a drop of blood that has fallen on the hanky. I must've stuck the needle in the tip of my finger. I never felt it. I don't cry — even when Mrs. Riley cuffs me for spoiling the work.

"Go and wash out the stain," she says, "and fetch me your boots, the ones you hide under your bed. I can sell them and they'll pay for your keep a bit longer. You heard me, girl. I want them now."

Next day she takes in a baby for me to mind, a thin little yellow-faced girl who screams all day. She sleeps in my old place in the bed, and I sleep wrapped in my shawl on the floor in the corner. I get up and rock the baby in the night when she wails. "Ta-ra-ra Boom-de-ay," I sing to her, and think of Helen — how we laughed that time, and the blood on her handkerchief. I wish I still had my boots.

One night, when Mrs. Riley has gone to bed, I put my shawl over my head, tuck my Lillie Langtry picture – the flower glued to the back of it – inside my dress, and run off.

Helen said to go to the big gray house, and I remember the way. I hurry down the alley, past the King's Head pub glowing warm and bright in the dark. The door is open and I see the sawdust on the floor, hear the piano playing, smell the beer. As I run by, a man stumbles out and pushes against me. I fall down. A Gypsy woman selling trinkets from her wooden tray puts her hand out to help me. The children waiting for their parents to come out of the pub call out: "Gypsy girl, tea leaf (thief), go to jail, won't get bail."

And then suddenly Bert is here – he must've followed me. He grabs my arm and says, "Ma'll kill you for running away." That's when I cry. He is pinching my arm; it hurts. I know I'll never see Helen again, and I have no one in the world to tell my troubles to.

All at once Bert lets go and starts howling, "Ow, get off me, you big bully. I never did nothing." I look up at a gentleman, not much taller than Bert, who is holding him by the collar so he can't get at me. I rub my sore arm, glad to be safe from Bert's cruel fingers.

"On your way, sharp, before I call the police," the gentleman says to Bert, who runs off as fast as a whippet.

"Thank you, sir," I whisper, wanting to get away.

"You're not very old to be out alone. Is your mother in there?" he asks, looking towards the pub door.

That's when I start to cry again. He seems so kind. I tell him about Helen and Mrs. Riley and Bert. I explain how Helen said I was to go to the big gray house, and how the people there look after children like me.

The man takes my hand and says, "I am Dr. Barnardo. Stepney Causeway is the place you are looking for. Come along with me; the home is only a short walk away. I am sure Matron can find some supper for you."

Well, he has nice eyes, but I don't go nowhere with strangers, so I ask him to make sure, "Are there words written over the door, sir?"

He looks at me very solemnly and says, "Indeed there are, and they are true because I wrote them: NO DESTITUTE CHILD EVER REFUSED ADMISSION."

So I go with him, and that's how I become a Barnardo's girl.

HALIFAX, NOVA SCOTIA, CANADA

June 2005

Carpenter's Rest

Grandfather's waiting at the airport. He hurries forward to give me a big hug. Every time I see him I think how alike he and Dad are, add or subtract a few wrinkles and gray hair.

"Is this all you've brought, Katie? I do admire a woman who travels light." He insists on carrying my case, even though it's on wheels. I refuse to let him take my backpack though.

"Here we are," he says, beaming proudly.

"You've bought a van? What happened to the this-will-last-forever station wagon? You worshipped it. That wagon was older than me."

"It was indeed, but much less beautiful." I roll my eyes at him.

Grandfather opens the door. "In you get, madam. This is our brand-new Dodge minivan, a more suitable vehicle for picking up guests. After all, the proprietor of an upscale bed-and-breakfast needs to drive something of distinction, don't you think?"

"It's great. New leather always smells so nice," I say. I lean my head back and close my eyes. I couldn't get to sleep last night. I didn't even finish packing until after midnight. This morning Step was throwing up – morning sickness, I guess – and Dad was fussing over her. By the time we got to the airport, there was a huge lineup. The plane was overbooked and I was switched from the window seat to a middle one and had elbows sticking into me the whole trip.

Dad and Step had to rush off to a different terminal, so there was really no time to say good-bye. "I'll call you, Katie, have fun. Give our love to the grandparents," Dad said. Naturally, love to everyone but me.

"We're almost there," Grandfather says.

"Sorry. You know how I always get sleepy in cars. Tell me about the house."

"It's an old Victorian mansion that was built in 1899 for a local sea captain, who drowned a few years later. It was bought by a merchant, a Mr. Macready, for his family. His daughter, Miss Elisabeth, lived there till quite recently. I met her when we signed the deeds, just before she moved into a nursing home nearby. She wagged her finger at me and said, 'Now be sure to take good care of my house, sir. And don't let the captain worry you. He does like to wander around the place on stormy nights, just to make sure that everything's shipshape.'"

"And does he?"

"Gran and I don't take any notice of rattles and creaks. Still, you never know, perhaps there is a resident ghost. I might put it on our website, to entice more visitors. What do you think?"

"A ghost? Awesome."

We pull up in front of a turreted house with freshly painted blue-and-white trim. "Here we are, Carpenter's Rest. Out you get."

Gran is waiting at the open door of the glassed-in storm porch. I run up the side steps and she puts her arms round me. "Welcome, Katie, come on in. Let me look at you. I promised myself I wouldn't say how much you've grown, but you have. Edward, look at this child – she's as tall as me. Was the flight awful? You look a bit wan. Starving, I expect. Air travel isn't the fun it used to be."

"I'm fine, Gran. Dad sends his love." I look around. There's a smell of lemon polish and lots of paneled wood and pretty wallpaper. "This is neat." Grandfather shuts the front door, making the crystal pendants on the chandelier chime gently.

"I'll give you a very quick tour, Katie, and then you can get settled in. Lunch will be ready in about half an hour, if you two can hold out that long," Gran says.

"I'm okay. They served a breakfast snack on the plane – a stale bun with some kind of pressed meat." Suddenly there's a lump in my throat. I'm thinking about what Dad would have said if I'd produced that on one of our stir-fry nights. I can actually hear his "I don't think so." The last couple of weeks have not been the greatest. . . .

Gran links her arm through mine. "This is the library. We've finally had the piano tuned. There are board games and lots of books, so our guests can have old-fashioned entertainment when they get through sight-seeing. Isn't the brick fireplace wonderful? Our own sitting room is next door. We can close the sliding doors if we don't want to be disturbed." We walk down the hall to the kitchen.

"Your grandfather and I eat in here usually. The dining room is too formal for the two of us. I plan to serve elegant breakfasts there when we open for business. All we need now is a little servant girl in a mobcap to make it really authentic."

Gran can be a bit overwhelming if you haven't seen her for a while.

"You're very quiet, Katie. Are you feeling jet-lagged? Come and take a peek at the garden. It almost makes you forget the busy world outside. I have to concentrate on the roses. Miss Macready let them get a bit wild. They need pruning."

I walk out onto the deck, which has big tubs of lavender under the kitchen and dining-room windows. "What do you think of my walled garden?" Gran asks. She doesn't wait for me to answer, but it's actually perfect – the way I imagine the Secret Garden looked. "We get all kinds of birds sheltering here," she continues. "They're as good as an alarm clock in the morning. Come upstairs now; I'm longing for you to see your room."

We walk up the spiral staircase. The sun shines through a rose-colored stained glass window. Even the wood glows pink. I hate pink. The back of my neck feels hot. I'm thirsty and tired and wonder what's for lunch.

"The main bedrooms are on this floor. *The Carpenter's* is ours and *A Garden View* and *The Lilac Room* are guest suites. Your room is on the top floor, traditionally where the servants, nanny, and children used to sleep. We thought you'd like the privacy. I'm just going to find some towels for you. Go on up, dear, your door's open."

I climb up the last few steps to a narrow hallway. There's a bathroom on one side, and three rooms next to each other with their names painted on tiles beside each door: *The Attic, Nursery,* and *Katie's Room.* I take a quick look into the first two. They're both empty except for tins of paint and rolls of wallpaper, stacked in the corners. The nursery is the biggest room and has bars across the window.

The door of my room is open. There's a window seat, which follows the curve of the wall. I can see the apple trees in the garden. One of them has a swing hanging from a thick branch. An old shed behind it is covered with climbing ivy.

A narrow wardrobe stands against one wall. A small chest of drawers, with a china basin and jug on it, stands against another, and, in a low alcove, there's a shabby old-fashioned trunk. I can just make out a couple of faded letters on the lid – an *I* and an *L*.

The single bed has a brass headboard. I pull my copy of *The Secret Garden* from my backpack and put it on the table beside my bed. That's what this room reminds me of. Almost everything does. This might be Martha the maid's room. That's the cane chair, where she'd fold her clothes at night, and in winter she'd shiver with cold, her bare feet glad of the cotton mat on the floor in front of the bed. The blue-and-white patchwork quilt might have been sewn by her mother, though I don't know how she'd have time with all those children to take care of – I think it was twelve.

Gran comes in with the towels over her arm. She picks up my book. "I loved that novel when I was your age. Still do."

"Me, too. We're doing it for the school play next term. This is a great room, Gran. Is that trunk one of Grandfather's bargains?" He loves going to auctions and flea markets.

"It belonged to your great-aunt Millicent. I use it for storing extra quilts and blankets. Are you ready to eat, Katie? Lunch will be spoiled if we don't go down and have it soon."

Grandfather sits at one end of the long kitchen table, tossing salad in a wooden bowl. Gran slices a baguette, and brings a brown earthenware casserole to the table.

"Cheese soufflé made with six eggs, especially in your honor, Katie. Help yourself."

I put some salad on my plate. "I think I'll stick to bread and salad." There's no way I'm going to eat that eggy stuff. I try not to look at it.

"Have just a little. Pass me your plate, dear."

"Gran, I guess I should have told you . . . I've sort of developed an aversion to eggs lately. I'll eat bread and salad, if that's alright."

"I've got some cold ham, or how about a piece of cheese? You're not dieting are you, Katie?"

I can't stand this interrogation. *When did Gran turn into someone so − I don't know − grandmotherly?* "I'm not dieting. Cheese is fine, thanks." I keep my eyes on my own plate while they eat their eggs. You can call it any-thing you like – soufflé, whatever – it's only dressed-up scrambled eggs.

Lunch is finally over. "I'm away to my workshop," Grandfather says. "I've got a sign to finish by tonight. I thought we'd have a house naming ceremony. I'll expect you to do the honors, Katie." He used to teach wood-working at the high school. He's really great at making things and refinishing stuff. "It was a delicious soufflé, Norah, my dear. My favorite."

I wish I'd gone to camp with Angie.

"It's warm enough to sit outside. Take this please, Katie." Gran hands me a plate of chocolate brownies and puts two glasses and a pitcher of lemonade on a tray. I hold the door open for her.

"Try that old rocking chair, dear – wonderfully relaxing. It used to belong to Mr. Macready. His daugh-ter told us she remembers her father sitting out here after dinner and smoking his cigars."

It seems ages since I left Toronto. Dad and Stephanie must be more than halfway to England by now. I sip my lemon-ade, and eat a brownie. "Good brownies, Gran."

"You always did like them. Now tell me what you've been up to. Is school going well? Are you and the lovely Stephanie getting along? It *is* exciting about the baby, isn't it? I'm sure you'll enjoy being a big sister."

A truthful answer is liable to give Gran a bit of a shock. "School's okay. I haven't thought much about the baby yet. It's not due till Christmas. Is it fun being retired?" *Brilliant Katie, change the subject.*

"Retired? We've never worked so hard in our lives. But I always wanted to run a bed-and-breakfast. We've already been getting inquiries."

"That's great. It's a terrific house. I'll go up and leave you in peace, Gran, and put my stuff away." I escape. I've got a bit of a headache.

Before supper Grandfather hammers the new driftwood sign into the front lawn. I take a deep breath and, feeling a bit like the queen naming a ship, say, "I name this house Carpenter's Rest. Bless all who live here."

"Well done, Katie. This calls for a toast." We go inside and he and Gran have champagne.

Dinner is by candlelight in the paneled dining room. There's a seafood pie, with chunks of Nova Scotia lobster and scallops in a cream sauce topped with mashed potatoes. I have two helpings.

A door bangs upstairs, making the candles flicker. I say, only half seriously, "Captain's making his rounds."

My grandparents tell me ghost stories. Gran says there's supposed to be a resident ghost in the Spring Garden Library. "It's rumored that the ghost is a former librarian who prowls the corridors, angry because she's been fired. I always hoped I'd see her, but I've never caught a glimpse."

"I think we might be in for a bit of a windstorm," Grandfather says. "I'll check the windows in a minute." He finishes his rice pudding.

I put down my spoon, and try to stifle a huge yawn. Gran suggests I go to bed. I offer to help with the dishes, but Grandfather says, "Go along, Katie. It's my turn tonight."

I run a bath in the deep claw-footed tub and soak for ages. When I finally get out, my bedroom is filled with moonlight. I sit on the window seat and look out at the garden.

When I was little, I'd kneel down beside my mother in our backyard and dig holes in the dirt, like Mary Lennox wanting her little "bit of earth." The swing moves back and forth in the wind. The moon dips down behind the shed. I climb into bed, too tired to read or write.

Wind billows the curtains into my room. A shadow appears on the wall of the alcove. . . . It looks like a girl holding a flower.

My mouth is too dry for me to cry out; my heart's pounding. I fumble for the switch and finally manage to turn the light on. The wall is blank. Everything is exactly the way it was this afternoon.

I jump out of bed, almost too afraid to let my feet touch the floor. I close the window and huddle under the quilt. *Grow up, Katie. Just because the house is old doesn't mean there's a ghost here. It was a shadow — that's all.* But I pull the quilt over my head and lie awake for hours.

HALIFAX, NOVA SCOTIA, CANADA

July 2005

William

Someone's calling my name, but the voice is a long way off: "Breakfast, Katie." A radio's on. There's a clatter of dishes. *At this hour?* It feels like the middle of the night. I roll over and go back to sleep and don't wake up again for hours.

My headache's gone and I'm starving. I jump out of bed and open the window wide and lean out. There are long tendrils of ivy creeping up the wall. *That's what I saw last night in the moonlight – ivy looking like arms, holding a flower.* It reminds me of the shadow puppets we used to make when I was small.

I check the alcove, run my fingers over the creamy wallpaper, and lift up the lid of the trunk, which is packed with neatly folded quilts. Not a ghost in sight.

There's a note for me downstairs, propped up against a jug of flowers on the kitchen table:

Good morning, Katie. Glad you had a good sleep. Orange juice in the fridge and cranberry muffins on the counter — eat as many as you like. I've gone for a walk in the Public Gardens. Grandfather's in the shed. He'd love a cup of coffee midmorning, if you can manage it. Fill the percolator half full of water and add two and a half scoops of coffee from the brown pottery container. Love, Gran.

Honestly, as if I can't make coffee . . . I've been making it for Dad since I was eight. I start the percolator and wolf down two muffins, which are delicious. The orange juice is freshly squeezed. After I'm done, I carry a mug of coffee down to the shed. The door's propped open. Grandfather's perched on a stool, gluing a tail on a beautiful old rocking horse with flashing eyes, black forelock and mane. I put the coffee beside him on the workbench, and sit down on an upturned barrel.

"Coffee smells good. Thanks, Katie. Handsome old fellow, isn't he?"

"Amazing. Where does he come from?"

"That's the astonishing thing. He was standing in that corner, covered with a piece of old sacking. I touched up his coat, gave him a new mane and tail, and he's good as new. How about giving me a hand?" Grand-father holds out a soft rag and a tin of saddle soap, and I start to polish the harness and saddle. He takes down the glue pot from the shelf. The whole shed looks like a miniature hardware store, with its assortment of paints, varnishes, tins of nails and polishes and dyes. He puts another dab of glue on the tail.

"Where's the horse going when he's finished?" I ask.

"I thought in the nursery, which is probably where he started out. One of these days that new grandchild of ours will ride him, and maybe our great-grandchildren. A wooden horse like this will last for another hundred years."

"I like that — stuff being passed down through the family. Like Great-aunt Millicent's trunk. I wish I knew more about her. I've only ever seen one faded photo. Why don't I know any stories about our family? It's like there's some deep dark secret that no one talks about. Is there?"

Grandfather looks up from his work. "Not really. You know that Millie passed away before you were born, and that she had to bring me up when Mother died."

"Yes. It's very sad. I'm sorry."

"I never knew Mother at all — I was just three days old when she died in 1935, so Millie was the closest thing to a mother I had. She was the eldest — only twelve years old — so she took over the running of the household:

my father, my ten-year-old brother, Hamish, and me. It
was the middle of the Great Depression, and there was
no money for hired help. Millie was forced to drop out
of school. She didn't complain, as far as I know, but it
can't have been much of a life."

"I wish I'd met her."

"I wish you had, too."

Grandfather hands me a brush and puts the tin of
varnish between us. "Let's start on the hooves and then
do the runners."

"Okay, but what about your father?"

Grandfather wipes the edge of his brush on the tin
and says, "My father, your great-grandfather William,
was an orphan, a Home boy who was sent to Canada
on the *Sardinia* in April 1907. I found his name on the
passenger list of Dr. Barnardo's boys in the National
Archives of Canada. The names for that year weren't
released until 2001."

"But why did you never tell us? Does my dad know?"

"No. My father never spoke much about his early
life. All we knew was that he had been born in England.
I guess he told us as much as he wanted us to know. He
worked long hours in the smithy. It can't have been easy
then to feed and clothe three children. Most families
were poor, struggling to make ends meet. I don't suppose
he was always paid on time for his labor. And we were

never the sort of family who sat around the table and exchanged confidences."

"So how did you find out?"

"Just before Dad passed away in 1970, Gran and I drove up to Truro to spend Sunday with him and Millie. It was one of those late warm days at the end of summer. Dad and I sat on the porch after lunch and Millie and Gran went for a walk, leaving Dad and me to drink our tea. He had a box of old horseshoes on the table beside him, and was sorting them. He could never bear to sit and do nothing."

"You're like that too, Grandfather."

"Like father like son, I suppose. I wondered what had made him choose to become a blacksmith. He was telling me about one of the horses, the worst kicker he'd ever shod. I think he remembered all of them.

"When your great-uncle Hamish died in World War II, it almost broke Dad's heart. My brother was only nineteen years old when he died in 1944. He'd joined the navy as soon as he'd finished his apprenticeship with Dad. They'd planned to expand the business after the war, making ornamental goods like wrought iron gates and light brackets as well as wagon wheels and shoeing.

"I asked him if he remembered the moment when he knew what he wanted to do with his life. I realized there might not be another chance for a real talk, for him to speak freely to me before it was too late. I must have asked the right question because my dad began to tell me his story, at least as much as he was willing to share with me. It was as if he'd been waiting all these years to speak:

"'My father, Albert Carr, worked with horses all his life. He was a stableman for a London horse bus company. One day he let me go with him to the stables. I watched him groom and feed the horses. "They'll never let you down if you treat them right," he said. Then he lifted me up onto the back of a big glossy brown mare. She twitched her ears and flicked her tail when I patted her neck. After I got down, Father took an apple out of his pocket and handed it to me. "Give it to the horse," he said. Not too many apples came my way, but it never entered my head to eat it myself. I've never forgotten that day – that was when I knew.

"'"Will we tell Frankie?" I asked him on the way home. Frankie was my brother, a year and a half younger than me. Father said Frankie would get his turn when he was a bit older. Frankie never did get his turn.

"'I was five years old in 1900, the year my father went off to South Africa to fight in the Boer War. "Don't you fret. I'm off to take care of

the colonel's horses," he said. He gave Frankie and
me a whole penny each and told us to look after
our mother. He turned at the door, saluted, and
then he was gone. He didn't come back.

"'We had to move from our neat little house
to a smaller one. Mother took in washing to eke
out the small pension she received as a soldier's
widow. Frankie and I helped as best we could. We
carried bucket after bucket of water from the
pump we shared with the other families in the
lane, and Mother heated the water on the kitchen
stove. She spent her days bent over a basin of hot
soapy water, scrubbing other people's soiled
clothes on the washboard. The kitchen walls ran
with steam. When the clothes were dry, Mother
ironed them with heavy flatirons.

"'Frankie and I delivered the laundry. Now
and then we made the odd copper shoveling
manure from the streets and selling it. We never
kept the money – it was for Mother. We tried to
look after her like Father had said we should.

"'Sometimes Mother sent us to the street
market on a Saturday to buy a head of cabbage.
While I bargained with the stall owner, Frankie
stuffed his pockets with carrots and onions. We
did what we had to do. We never thought of it
as stealing.

" 'There were many days when we all went to bed without supper. Mother often didn't finish her meal. "You have mine, boys," she'd say, "I'm not feeling hungry."

" 'One day Frankie and I got home and emptied our pockets of bits of coal we'd manage to scrounge from the back of the coal delivery carts. Mother made us wash our hands before she let us sit down to the soup she'd made. I saw that there was a bit of bacon in our bowls, as well as potato and onion. "For a treat," Mother said.

" 'After we'd scraped our bowls clean, she told us we had to be brave. "I've sold everything I can and there still isn't enough to pay this month's rent." That was when I noticed that Father's chair had gone. "You both need boots, and Frankie's too thin. I'll have to go into service. Barnardo's Home will take you in. It won't be for long, just till I get on my feet." I was nine years old, and I wanted to believe her.

" 'At the orphanage, Frankie clung to her skirts and cried like a baby. They told us Mother was allowed to visit in three months' time and we could write to her once a month. Then she signed a paper, kissed us good-bye, and was gone. The big door closed behind us and I couldn't stop thinking that Frankie and me were on the wrong side of it. Father had said to look after her.

" 'After Mother left, a doctor checked us over – eyes, ears, chests. He wore a white coat, and wrote things down. Our hair was clipped short. We were told to scrub in the bath and to dress in new clothes and boots made in the Home's own workshop. That evening we sat at long tables in the dining hall, eating bread and dripping, drinking cocoa, and looking exactly like all the other orphans.

" 'Later, in the big dormitory where over a hundred boys of all ages slept in tidy rows, I whispered to Frankie, "You and me, we aren't like them, Frankie. We're not orphans."

" 'We soon got used to the discipline and routine of the orphanage. Every morning we scrubbed, polished, mopped, and swept. If it wasn't done right, we did it all over again. And it had to be finished before we were allowed to eat our breakfast of bread and tea. Then there were lessons and, in the afternoon, we learned a trade – carpentry or shoe making, upholstering, printing, or tailoring.

" 'Every minute was planned. We were never alone. On Sunday there was church, but there was also a pudding if we'd behaved ourselves all week. If we broke the rules, we got beaten and every boy was made to watch. It wasn't all bad – we ate three meals a day. Christmas was the best time; we got an orange, and there was a tree.

"'For the first two years, Mother came to see us every visiting day. One morning, when I was eleven, I was called into the superintendent's office. Frankie was in the country by this time as a foster family had been found for him. The doctor'd said he had a weak chest and wanted him to have fresh air. Frankie wrote that they let him keep rabbits.

"'I was glad Frankie wasn't there when they told me Mother had passed away. I was allowed to stay in the dormitory all that day. "Be brave. It's for the best," they told me. *How could it be for the best?* I thought. I wrote and told Frankie. I said that one day we'd be together, and he was to get well.

"'Every year the orphanage sent boys overseas. They had to make room for the new boys coming in. That's what all our training was for: to get us ready to take our places in the world, especially the New World.

"'One day, just before my twelfth birthday, we were summoned into the dining hall to listen to a talk about Canada. "Good generous families are waiting eagerly, boys, to take you in. Are you ready for the challenge, lads? Are you ready to work and make us proud of you?" I thought, *Isn't that what we've been doing? Haven't we all been working from morning to night?*

"'I never took my eyes from the man who had the power to put us on the Canada list, or to leave us here for another year. "Only the very best are chosen for the greatest adventure of your lives," he said. "Canada is a fine country with great mountains and rivers and wildlife. In winter you will skate across frozen lakes; in summer the trees are heavy with fruit waiting to be picked. Who wants to go?" Almost every boy put up his hand.

"'The man said, "Our founder, Dr. Barnardo, would be proud of you. 'The flower of the flock,' he used to say, 'we are sending the flower of the flock.'" He wrote down our names and that's how I got on the list.

"'Frankie and his new parents came down to London to say good-bye to me. Frankie gave me a packet of toffee. I stuffed a piece into my mouth, so I'd have an excuse not to speak for a minute. I had such a lump in my throat. Before they left, I promised to write. I watched them go, and suddenly I was filled with hope. We were on our way to a big new country! There'd be horses and farms. I could be anything I wanted to be. I knew people didn't adopt big boys of twelve, though I wasn't very tall for my age, and I was skinny. But if I was a foster boy, wouldn't I be like one of the family? Frankie might come out for a visit.

"'We had a fine send-off. New clothes and boots to wear, and trunks made in our own workshop. Inside there was a bible and a hymn book and work clothes, as well as an outfit for Sunday. A marching band played as we walked to the Barnardo Special – the train that took us to the Liverpool docks. A crowd of people cheered us on as we went up the gangway of the *Sardinia* – the ship on which we were to sail to Canada.

"'Over a hundred and fifty boys and almost the same number of girls, dressed in red-and-gray outfits, left England that day. They kept the boys and girls separate. Most of the time we were too seasick to give the girls a thought. We couldn't even enjoy the meals served to us by the stewards in their white jackets. The sea is rough in April, so you can imagine the stench down in steerage, where we slept. However sick we felt, it was up at six for a wash and prayers and breakfast.

"'I went on deck as much as I could, looking over the railings at the dark Atlantic, hoping I'd be the first to spot the icebergs they'd told us about, and dreaming of the horses I'd ride through the meadows. I planned my first letter to Frankie, so that he'd know I was having a good life too.

"'One morning, about a week after the ship left England, I was on deck as usual. I'd become accustomed to the rolling of the ship by now. The wind was blowing hard, and waves spilled onto the deck. I had to grip the railings to keep my balance. My lips tasted of salt, and I shouted words into the wind just for the joy of being there, being part of all that sky and water and open space.

"'Not far from me I saw a girl. I don't know why I hadn't noticed her earlier. She was kneeling down on deck, as if searching for something she'd lost in the ocean. The hem of her skirt was soaked. I knew she must be one of the orphan girls because of her red cloak. She'd get in trouble for that, I thought –'"

"Edward, Katie, I'm back. You shouldn't be inside on such a lovely day. I've made sandwiches for lunch. Let's eat in the garden."

I feel dazed, as if I've been right inside the story, kneeling down and looking into the sea. Gran's voice breaks the spell. . . .

That night, before I go to sleep, I read about Mary Lennox leaving India for England. It doesn't describe the voyage, which took ages in those days, or how scared she must have been going to a strange country to live with an uncle she'd never met.

I dream about a ship and a girl who's alone, but it's all mixed up. I don't know if it's about me, or Mary, or the orphan girl in Great-grandfather's story.

In the dream the girl talks to her mother, the way I used to.

THE ATLANTIC OCEAN

April 1907

Sardinia

I wish you hadn't gone to Heaven -- I wish you were here with me, Helen. That day on the bridge, the day of my birthday, you looked down at the ships on the River Thames and said you wanted to sail across the ocean. And now it's me who's here instead of you.

I did everything just the way you said I should. After I ran away from Mrs. Riley, they took me in at the orphanage. The doctor said, "Girls do better away from the distractions of the city," and sent me to The Girls' Village Home in Essex. That's in the country. Did you ever go to the country, Helen?

I don't know how you'd have put up with the quiet, but it was lovely, like living in a park. Trees and flowers and lawns all around the Home, and the girls lived in little cottages. When I first saw them, I thought they looked like the doll's house you told me Miss Sadie played with.

All the cottages were named after flowers. Mine was called Rose. There were sixteen girls in our house. We made sure that we kept the rooms bright, shiny, and beautiful, like the hair ribbons we wore to church on Sundays. The ribbons were the colors of flowers. Mine was white. I brought it with me to wear for special occasions in Canada.

There was a housemother to take care of the girls and she was always an unmarried lady. We slept four to a room, and we each had our own bed. We did all the housework – I wish you could have seen how spotless we kept that little cottage.

I liked being one of the older girls who looked after the little ones. We had lessons and went to church and Sunday school, and learned to wash and cook and iron and sew, ready to earn a living. Girls were always coming and going – some fostered out in the village, some left to work as scullery maids in big houses, others were shipped off to Canada.

I was lucky at first because our housemother, Miss Bruce, took a liking to me and treated me nicely. She chose me to serve her meals in the parlor. Our food was sent over from the big kitchen in the main house, but the housemother didn't eat with us. She ate meat almost every day, and little pies. Once Miss Bruce gave me a slice of beef from the roast she kept on her pantry shelf.

We hardly ever had meat so I shared it with Maria, who was always hungry.

I felt sorry when Miss Bruce left us to go and look after her sister in Scotland, who'd had a fall. That's what they told us, but some of the girls said she'd got a sweetheart, and was going to get married.

Then, last year, there were changes. Right from the first day, I got on the wrong side of Miss Dodds. I had gone into her parlor to do the dusting. I did knock, but she didn't hear me. I saw her drinking from a bottle of medicine. She smelled the way Mrs. Riley did on a Friday night, or on payday. Miss Dodds screamed at me: "Get out, get out!" She never let me set foot in her parlor again. Susanna became her favorite – a pretty little blonde girl, meek as a mouse, and afraid of her own shadow.

There was nothing I could do to please Miss Dodds. She shouted at me right in front of the little girls, and they started to disobey me, and I'd get in more trouble.

I don't think girls should be pinched and slapped for something that they can't help, do you, Helen? One day Miss Dodds tied my left arm behind my back because she saw me favoring my left hand over my right. Another time she noticed that Maria smiled at me in church, and that I smiled back. We weren't talking, but she punished us both – we had to go without pudding for Sunday supper for the rest of the month.

One day a lady came to talk to us about Canada. It sounded lovely. I thought about all those nice people waiting for us to be part of their family, and the fresh air and good food and having time to pick berries and flowers. You always said we should aim for something better, so I put up my hand to go, like most of the girls. I expected we'd have to work hard, but I didn't mind that. I wanted to be treated fair.

I don't even know what it's like, being part of a family. I've only watched families from the outside, going to church, or walking together.

I sang in the Barnardo choir. I love to sing – learned that from you, didn't I? Last year, they took us up to London to perform at a concert in aid of Dr. Barnardo's children. Imagine me singing at the Royal Albert Hall, in front of thousands of people. The king and his beautiful queen, Alexandra, sat in the royal box, listening to us. It was a lovely night – just like magic.

The boys went onstage first, showing all the work they'd do when they got to Canada. They cut logs, shoveled snow, fed the animals, loaded hay, and baked bread. Then it was the girls' turn. We mimed washing, hanging up clothes, and ironing.

It sent shivers up my spine when those ladies and gentlemen, in their fine clothes, stood up to sing the national anthem with us:

God save our gracious King,
Long live our noble King,
God save the King.

The money people paid that night was to send the
Waifs and Strays to Canada. That's what they called us,
Waifs and Strays. Makes us sound like dogs, doesn't it?

I'm going so far away, Helen. I hope good times start
soon because there's rats running over our feet where we
sleep, down below in steerage, and the smell is awful
there. *Never mind*, I tell myself, *we're almost halfway*. I
think about going to a nice family, like they promised us.
Would you believe I have my own trunk, with clothes
for work and a dress for Sundays? I've got the picture
postcard and my flower safe, so I'm all set, Helen. It's just
that my stomach feels funny, the way it did the day you
first showed me Stepney Causeway. Of course, I didn't
know then it was an orphanage.

That boy standing further down the deck is staring
at me. I can see him out of the corner of my eye. I've seen
him before. He's coming over. I pretend not to notice.

"What are you looking at?" he asks me. "Be careful
you don't get washed overboard."

I'd know him anywhere – he's thin and his face is all
bones. If they let his hair grow longer, it'd be fair and flop

over his forehead. Last year, when he was running off-
stage at the Royal Albert Hall, he dropped his cap. The
choir was waiting to file on, and I was in the front. I
picked it up and gave it to him. He flushed red, and said,
"Thanks, miss." It's not often they let us even near a boy.

"What's it to you, then?" I say, looking up at him.

"I can't swim, and there's no one near to fish you
out." He has a nice smile. "I spoke to you at the Royal
Albert Hall, remember? You handed me my cap on
concert night."

"So I did. Are you glad to be going off to Canada?"

"I am. I hated the home. Everything about it − the
rules, the food, the way they made us watch the beatings,
if someone tried to run away. Beat them half to death. It's
not right. There was never a minute to think your own
thoughts. I hated sharing a dormitory with a hundred and
fifty boys, and I miss my brother, Frankie. He's been
adopted." He looks away. I don't think he meant to tell
me that much. He hardly knows me. I like talking to him.

"Do you want to know why I'm looking at the
ocean?" I say. "It is because I can't abide those waves,
taking us away from everything we know. Don't they
have orphans of their own in Canada?"

"Not like us, they don't. We're the best there is.
Didn't you hear we're 'the flower of the flock'?"

I laugh with him then, and a great big wave slops
over the deck, drenching us both. I try to stand up and

almost fall, but the boy grabs my elbow and steadies me. I can see my friend Maria waving to me, circling her arms. She's on the far side of the ship, playing with the other girls.

"I'd better go. They want me to turn the skipping rope for them."

"Good-bye, Flower," he says.

I toss my head, the way you used to, Helen, and try to walk gracefully across the slippery deck because I know he's watching me.

Twenty-four hours after seeing our first icebergs, we get ready to set foot on Canadian soil. They tell us we are entering Halifax harbor. Everyone is on deck waiting, dressed in clean clothes, washed and brushed and looking as good as we can manage after almost two weeks at sea. All we can see is fog. It's just like London, only it doesn't smell full of dirt and smoke. It smells of sea and salt.

Sometimes at the home in Essex, after days of rain, the sun would break through the clouds, a watery sun followed by a rainbow. I wish for the sun now and, just as the ship comes close to the shore, the fog lifts. I can see the top of hills and, below, a scattering of houses. It's a magic city floating in the sky.

This would be a lovely place to live. I watch the seabirds swoop so free out of the mist. They call to each other. *One day I'll come back here*, I promise myself,

Our ship, the *Sardinia*, docks and we walk two by two down the gangway behind Miss Mackay, the superintendent who has looked after us on the journey.

"Doesn't this make you think of that story about Noah and his ark – the one they read us in Sunday school?" I ask Maria.

"Do you mean, we're like animals?" Maria and I love a joke. Our legs are so wobbly we have to hold on to each other to stay upright. The wind makes our cloaks billow round us, and we try to hold them down. Eileen, Maria's little sister, is in front of us, clutching hands with another small girl.

Waiting in line to be admitted to our new country, we shiver in the cold of the immigration shed. I dread the inspection by the doctor. I know it will hurt when he rolls back my eyelid to check for disease, but I'm determined not to make a sound.

Eileen is next. Her eyes are infected. We hear the doctor say "trachoma" to the nurse. Eileen sobs, clinging to Maria, and hides her face in her sister's skirt. The nurse pulls the girl away, and leads her off. She'll be sent back to England.

"I can't let her go alone. What shall I do, Lillie?" Maria implores me.

"Rub your knuckles in your eyes to make them red. Tell the doctor your eyes itch. Hurry, it's your turn after me."

I smile at the doctor, even when he pulls both eyelids almost inside out. I'm waved through. I hear Maria tell him her eyes feel as though they're full of grit and itch constantly. He keeps her back, and she joins her sister.

Maria smiles at me and mouths her thanks. I'm sad to lose a friend, but we'd be unlikely to be sent to the same place anyway. Miss Mackay says they'll have another chance to come over when they're better as British orphans are in great demand. Then she counts us, and we hurry to the train that's waiting to take us to Dr. Barnardo's Home for Girls in Peterborough.

The train is part of the Grand Trunk rail line. I don't know what's grand about it, Helen. The seats are wooden, and so hard I'd be surprised if they don't leave ridges across our backs. You wouldn't like them one bit.

The journey goes on and on. I'm too tired to sleep. Instead I decide to pay attention to the country I've come to live in. I want to like it here.

Through the window I see a huge world of sky and fields and lakes. Houses are built far away from each other, surrounded by a few outbuildings. Horses, cows, and sheep graze peacefully. I think you could walk here forever without ever meeting another human being. If only you were with me. . . .

★

After the first day and night on the train, I don't care whether we end up in China or Africa, just so long as we stop moving.

The train comes to a halt at last. The guard calls out, "Peterborough." We've arrived, and almost tumble down the high steps, we are so eager to be on firm ground. Porters push carts piled high with luggage; gentlemen smoking fat cigars accompany ladies wearing elegant hats. Children and nursemaids, errand boys and merchants crowd the platform.

We line up neatly behind Miss Mackay and I pretend not to notice the curious stares. Outside the station entrance, horse-drawn carriages are waiting to take us to the Girls' Home.

The road is muddy, and there are wooden boardwalks. Not like the cobblestones we walked on in the village at home. I'm not complaining, Helen, I'm just taking notice of what's different here. A streetcar rattles by and the gas lamps are bright enough for me to read some of the signs over the shops: GILMOUR'S BAKED GOODS (wouldn't I just love to go in there this very minute and buy a meat pie for us to share?); HOOPER'S CONFECTIONERY (so tempting – not that I've any money to spend!); FOWLER'S ICE-CREAM PARLOR (did you and Mr. Charles ever eat ice cream? I've never tasted it, but when I do I'll tell you about it).

The horses turn into a wide drive – we have arrived at last. Miss Mackay says Dr. Barnardo's Home for Girls used to be called Hazelbrae, which I think is a much prettier name. The grounds are beautiful, with fine trees, lawns, and shrubberies. The rose brick house is three stories high, with a porch running along the front. Wide pillars are set at intervals, and make the house look very imposing. I have never liked big houses; they make me afraid. Well, we are not here for long as I shall be going to my new family soon. I wish Maria had stayed. I would feel less strange with an old friend from the Village Home beside me.

Two girls show us up to a long dormitory, with rows and rows of narrow beds. We are told to wash and then go to the dining hall. I never cry, Helen, well, hardly ever, but it's all I can do to suppress my tears and swallow my supper of soup, bread, and cocoa. Then we are sent to bed. No one feels like talking. For all its grand looks, it's just another orphanage.

I lie down between clean sheets, my head on a soft white pillow, but I am unable to sleep. I pretend it is Sunday, a Sunday long ago, Helen. You have come to take me for a walk along the Thames. We sit on the bench overlooking the river. I am so tired and I put my head on your lap. I fall asleep, feeling your hand softly stroking my cheek.

Morning arrives too quickly. After prayers, we make our beds before eating a breakfast of tea and oatmeal, which is the Canadian name for porridge.

We do chores. I've just finished sweeping the dining hall floor, and my hands are still damp from wiping down the wooden tables, when my name is called to go to Matron's office. A girl shows me the way. Luckily my apron is clean. I smooth my hair and follow her. She points to a door. I knock nervously. *Can my new family be here already to take me home?*

A voice calls, "Enter."

Miss Humphrey, the matron, is seated at her desk. Through the tall windows behind her, I see the sweep of lawns and the great elm trees that shade the porch. A bright fire burns in the hearth. Standing on one side of the fireplace is Miss Mackay, and seated in a high-backed chair facing Matron is a lady wearing a black dress, with lace trim around the neck and sleeves. She wears a large black-and-purple hat, and stares at me appraisingly, her light blue eyes cold. Her gray hair is scraped back under her hat. Two deep lines run from her nose to her thin pale lips. I don't think we're going to take to each other, Helen, though it is not my place to "venture an opinion," as Miss Mackay would say if she could read my thoughts.

Matron says, "Mrs. Dunn, this is Lillian Bridges.

Mrs. Dunn is the proprietress of a boarding house on Water Street."

I bob a curtsy and say, "Good morning, ma'am. It's Lillie, please, Matron." Miss Mackay silences me with a look, and Matron ignores my interruption, as if I'm an insect that's buzzed in by mistake.

"The girl has been with Barnardo's since the age of seven, and is thoroughly trained in domestic duties. She will be twelve in September, therefore she is required to complete two more years of school." I keep my eyes lowered.

When I first went to Barnardo's, they asked me how old I was. Well, I knew that, but I had no idea exactly *when* I'd turned seven. I remembered the day you took me out, Helen, and gave me a present because you said it was my birthday. The leaves on the trees were beginning to change color – crimson and gold – all along the Thames' embankment, but what day was that? Mrs. Riley lived at number four, so when they asked me the date of my birthday, I said September 4th, and that's what they wrote down.

Mrs. Dunn makes up her mind in a hurry, Helen. She stands up and shakes out her skirts. "I'll take her. The buggy's waiting outside."

I smile at her, even though I feel like a piece of goods that's just been purchased. "Thank you, ma'am," I say.

Matron tells me to fetch my cloak and that she'll have my trunk brought down.

When we settle into the buggy, Mrs. Dunn speaks rapidly to me: "My sister, Miss Alice Phipps, cooks for our establishment, and you will assist her in the kitchen, as well as serving at table and cleaning the boarders' rooms and the rest of the house. At present we have five permanent guests. There is a kitchen garden, which you will help tend, and we keep poultry, so there are always fresh eggs. You will be in charge of feeding the chickens, cleaning the henhouse, and collecting and washing the eggs. The *Almanac* says eggs must always be collected in daylight hours. A woman comes in on Mondays for the heavy wash. You will help her with the mangling, and do the ironing. I presume you are able to patch and darn?"

I manage to nod, hoping there wouldn't be too much mending. "I try my best, ma'am."

"Where are you from? You look very dark."

"I'm from London, ma'am. My mother told me my father came from Malta and I take after him. I never knew him. He died when I was a baby."

"And what did your mother do – stay at home and look after the household?"

"Yes, ma'am, she took care of the house." That isn't a lie; that's what a servant does. *Why is she asking all these questions? We're orphans, we lived in the orphanage – there's nothing more to tell.*

She starts talking again. *Doesn't she ever stop?*

"The most important thing a girl in domestic service possesses is her good name. Her character must be unblemished. I expect obedience without question, cleanliness in habits, and, above all, hard work. You will take the next few months to become accustomed to our ways, and in the fall you may go to school if you are still in my employ. On Sundays you will attend St. John's Anglican Church and Sunday school. St. John's is the oldest church in Peterborough — we are fortunate that we live close by."

The buggy stops in front of a pale yellow brick house with high narrow windows. I climb out after Mrs. Dunn, and she motions me to follow the driver, who carries my trunk to the rear of the house. "I will see you in the kitchen in a few moments," Mrs. Dunn says, and walks up the steps to her front door.

If I'm still in her employ, she said. I'm to be a skivvy! Why did they tell us we were going to be part of a family? Was it all lies to make room for more orphans in the home?

If you were standing beside me, Helen, what would you say? I know . . . roll up my sleeves, get to work, and do the best I can. I will, Helen, and I'll make you proud of me. You'll see.

HALIFAX, NOVA SCOTIA, CANADA

July 2005

Journey

The three of us start working on the top floor today. Grandfather's whitewashing *The Attic*, and Gran and I strip off the final layer of the nursery wallpaper. Dad called from England just after breakfast. Said Step sends her love to everyone.

I tug viciously at a piece of wallpaper that sticks stubbornly to the wall. I'm stubborn, too. I manage to peel it off, and begin on the next strip.

Gran says, "I remember, when you were small, I made you take a nap in the afternoon. You were not at all pleased. 'I don't take naps anymore,' you said. 'I have quiet times.' When I came back about half an hour later, you'd managed to pick off a corner strip of your new bedroom wallpaper. 'It came loose,' you told me, and you tried to put it back with spit."

"I'd forgotten all about that." I tear another long strip and watch it curl up like apple peel in one unbroken spiral.

"I must have made a lot of mistakes, Katie. It was a difficult time."

"I must have been a horrible kid." I really don't want to get talking about after Mom died. "Gran, I'd like to go and see Miss Macready. She must be pretty ancient by now. I want to ask her about living here as a child, the kind of stuff that might help me with the play. You know, how kids were brought up, what they played, did she garden? Did she have a nanny or a maid?"

Deep down I'm still wondering about that shadow on the wall. I haven't really convinced myself it was ivy. *Can moonlight make a bunch of leaves turn into the shape of a girl holding a flower?* And that weird mixed-up dream I had last night, I wish I could remember more. *Why do dreams always disappear the minute you wake up?*

It's no good discussing it with Gran — she'd fuss and think I was scared or homesick, and move me downstairs. I love my Secret Garden room, but there is something mysterious going on. Suppose, long ago, someone was unhappy or in trouble. Miss Macready might know if there was a secret. Kids always find things out.

Gran says, "Miss Elisabeth Macready must be at least ninety-six years old. She was a small child when her parents moved here in 1909. That's certainly the era of *The Secret Garden*. Why don't I give the Bide Awhile Nursing Home a call, and check about visiting hours?"

"Bide Awhile? What a creepy name for a seniors' home. That's like saying, 'You won't be here for long.' What our principal would refer to as 'sending the wrong message.'"

"I don't think that was the intention! I'll get cleaned up and make that call."

Grandfather and I go for a walk down to the harbor after lunch. Gran stays behind to carry on with the sampler she's stitching for the library: *Home Sweet Home*, the exact opposite of how I feel about mine right now.

We buy vanilla and chocolate ice-cream cones and eat them sitting on the boardwalk. I have to shoo away the gluttonous seagulls circling over our heads.

"I dreamt about the girl on the ship last night, the one in your father's story. Did they ever meet again? I hope so. Tell me everything that happened after they got to Canada."

"Dad told me more than I ever expected to hear him say that day, but there were some things he kept to himself. From what I've read about the Home children, they got on with their lives and didn't talk much about the past. They weren't all orphans — some were sent away without their parents' consent; some had parents who were destitute, or who didn't want them; some were runaways living on the streets of cities like Liverpool and Manchester and London, who were picked up by the authorities and sent overseas. Many children were overworked and underfed. I'm sure some wished they'd stayed in England.

"Dad said that when they finally set foot on Canadian soil, not very far from where we're sitting now, Katie, they passed through the immigration sheds. A few of the boys were met by farmers and driven off clinging to the sides of carts or buggies, heading into the unknown, while the rest climbed on board the train bound for Toronto and to points west. The girls were on the same train, but traveled in separate carriages. My father said:

"'I hoped I might catch a glimpse of the girl I'd talked to on the ship. I turned and waved, in case she was looking out of the train window. I wished I'd asked her name, and told her mine. The boy behind elbowed me to hurry up the steps. "Who are you waving at, you daft fool?" he jeered. I put my foot out to trip him.

"'"Why don't you look where you're going?" I said.

"'When we finally arrived in Toronto, we were taken to the Barnardo Home for Boys on

Farley Avenue. The minute we were through the doors, they checked us again for lice and disease.

" 'The one disease we all shared was fear. We'd come such a long way, and now we waited for one more destination, waited for what they'd promised us: a family to take us in. Was it going to come true? We'd already heard rumors of boys running away because they'd been badly treated. That night, lying awake in the dormitory, I could hear the sound of muffled weeping.

" 'Next morning Mr. Owen, the superintendent, told me I was going to a farm in Lindsay. He wrote down the address: *Jack Mitchell, Angeline, Lindsay, Ontario.* I didn't even know how to pronounce the name! I was given a lunch and sent on my way.

" 'I sat up on the train, rigid with anxiety, terrified I'd miss my stop. I was hardly able to take in the pretty countryside, dotted with lakes and rivers. I needn't have worried. The guard called out, "Lindsay," in a loud voice, and moments later I was standing beside my new tin trunk, on a platform bustling with life. Trains came and went, and people jostled to greet new arrivals, to pass the time of day, or to find their seats before the next departure. I had no idea what I was supposed to do. It was the first time in years I hadn't been part of a crowd of boys, herded from one place to another, obeying rules and regulations. I was on my own, bewildered and uncertain.

"'How would Mr. Mitchell know me? I'd been told I was to be met, but suppose he forgot – how would I get to the farm? I made sure the name tag pinned to my jacket was facing out. Then I hauled my belongings to the steps beside the station entrance, so anyone going in or out would notice me.

"'Once or twice people looked my way, but no one stopped to speak. The cold seeped through my boots. I must have waited two hours or more. At last a burly man, whom I'd noticed tying up his horse and buggy and who'd come down the steps to speak to the stationmaster, walked up to me. I jumped to my feet, and whipped off my cap, "Mr. Mitchell, sir? I'm William Carr, your boy from the orphanage."

"'"My boy?" He laughed, mocking me. "I don't have a boy, only a houseful of girls." He laughed again, enjoying his little joke. Then he walked all around me. If he'd carried a pitchfork, I swear he would have prodded me with it.

"'"I've changed my mind. You're too small. My pigs weigh twice what I do and they'd gobble you up in no time." He roared with laughter at the prospect. "I've had a word with the station-master – you can go back on the next train."

" "Please, sir, I'm strong, and pigs don't scare me." I hoped Mr. Mitchell wouldn't guess that the nearest I'd ever been to a pig was the rare occasion I'd tasted a pork sausage, or looked at a pig's head on a slab in the window of a butcher's shop in London. But to be sent back would be a disgrace.

" "My nephew's been sent for from out West. The wife decided she doesn't want anyone who isn't kin around the place." Then he turned his back on me and walked away.

" 'It had all been a game. He'd made up his mind long before he even spoke to me.

" 'I tore off my name tag and shoved it in my pocket. I swore I'd never go back to the orphan-age. They'd sent me to Canada for a better life, and I was resolved to find it.

" "I asked the stationmaster if he'd let me leave my trunk in the baggage room while I looked around the town, and he said that would be fine.

" 'Outside the station, porters were handing luggage up the steps of a high-wheeled horse-drawn bus, with BENSON'S HOTEL written on the side. I watched the horses struggling to turn into the muddy main street. Horses! Surely there would be a job in some stable for a boy who wanted to work with horses. I set off to find myself a place.

"'I walked down Kent Street, and in the next couple of hours I'd called in at six or seven livery stables attached to the hotels. None of them needed a stable boy. At Hamilton's Carriageworks, a boy cleaning some harnesses told me to try the forge behind Queen's Square. He'd heard the apprentice had gone back to his home in Bobcaygeon. I crossed the wide muddy street. The mud slopped up to my ankles and over my boots.

"'The smith was shoeing a horse. I stood at the entrance feeling the heat of the fire and watching the sparks fly into the dusk, like fireflies on a summer night. The blacksmith cradled the horse's front foot in his lap, starting with the heel of the shoe, loosening it gently before he removed the old nails with his pincers. Then he cleaned out the mud and gravel before fitting the new shoe. When he picked up the hind foot, the horse shifted about. Horses do that because they can't see what's going on. The blacksmith talked to him quietly, slid his hand down the horse's leg to the fetlock, picked up the foot and swung his knee under the horse, holding the upturned hoof in his lap ready to shoe. The smith had positioned himself so that even if the horse did kick, he could step away without getting hurt.

"'When the horse was shod, the blacksmith straightened up. He watched the owner lead the mare away and looked at me, waiting patiently to see what I wanted. I had a feeling that I had found what I was looking for. This might be my only opportunity to speak up for myself, and my future in the New World.

"'"My father worked with horses, and so did my grandfather," I blurted. I hadn't planned what I was going to say, but it all came pouring out: about the orphanage and leaving Frankie behind and being turned down by Mr. Mitchell and how this was the life I'd always wanted – to work around horses and one day to be a blacksmith like him.

"'He handed me a broom. I swept that forge as if my life were at stake, and in a way it was. I gathered the old horseshoes, adding them to a barrel already filled with other discarded shoes. I picked up bent nails, found some wood to chop, and stacked it near the furnace. When the forge was tidy, I stood the broom back in the corner.

" ' "You must keep that fire going, morning and night. Make sure it never goes out," he said.

" 'Yes, sir, I won't. I promise."

" 'The blacksmith struck the anvil with his big hammer so that it rang out like a bell – the sign that work was ended for the day. He shifted the hammer to his left hand, and held out his right for me to shake.

" ' "I'm Joseph Armstrong," he said.

" ' "My name is William Carr," I answered.

" 'Then he took me into the house for supper, and that's how my five-year apprenticeship began. We worked twelve- or fourteen-hour days for six, sometimes seven, days a week. We fixed wagon wheels and cutting knives, made bolts and hinges, forged ax handles, and mended sled runners. Mr. Armstrong made his own nails because they lasted longer than the ones turned out by machines. But over half the work we did was shoeing.

" 'A couple of months after I'd started working for Mr. Armstrong, Jack Mitchell brought his horse in to be shod. He looked at me, and said, "It's you, is it? I heard Mr. Armstrong took you on. How's the Home boy making out here? Giving you any trouble, Joe?"

" ' "I'll need you to walk the horse round, William, so I can see what's required," Mr.

Armstrong told me. When he'd taken a good look at the horse, and I had brought him back into the forge, Mr. Armstrong said, "My new apprentice will shoe your horse, Jack." Then he added, "The boy has good hands." I must have grown at least half an inch taller when I heard that. Compliments were rare in my life.

" 'It took me two hours to shoe the horse – a job Mr. Armstrong would have finished in half the time – but he never said a word, just grunted now and then to encourage me.

" 'Bit by bit I became part of the rhythm of the forge. Mr. Armstrong taught not through words – there were few of those – but through example. By the time I was a striker, the second pair of hands at the anvil, we worked as one and the same person. I rarely missed when he pointed with his hammer to where I was to strike next.

" 'At first I was given the worst jobs – that was how you learned. Apprentices were expected to handle the kickers, the nervous bad-tempered horses who kicked out when they were shod. Mr. Armstrong told me I had a way of talking to them that calmed them down, that I had the right way with troublesome animals. "A horse is like a human; he needs kindness," he said.

" 'When I was fourteen, I was paid my first wage of a dollar a month. I've never felt richer in my life. I banked most of it. I was too busy to spend it, except when the circus came to town. Everyone turned out for it: the procession headed by the elephants and the show afterwards. But I was always glad to get back to the forge. It made me feel uneasy looking at the mangy wild animals in their cramped cages.

" 'I remembered the girl on the boat, the way she'd gripped the rails. Sometimes I'd look up when I saw a girl with dark curls pass by, or heard a laugh that reminded me of her.

" 'I stayed with Joe and his wife until 1914, the year after my apprenticeship ended. In September, a month after World War I broke out, I went to the armory on Queen Square and volunteered for the army, hoping to be sent to a cavalry regiment. "Come back safe, Will," Joe said.

" 'We embarked for England, where we were to receive training before they sent us to France. I was anxious to see my brother again. I managed to have one leave with him. Frankie joined up the following year. I never saw him again; he died in France, at the Battle of Vimy Ridge in 1917. After the war, I returned to Canada and married your mother.'

"Dad refused to say another word on the subject after that and retreated into his customary silence. But we should be getting home. Gran will wonder where we've got to."

"The story sounds like it happened yesterday," I say. I'm full of questions, but I can tell Grandfather has closed up too, exactly like his dad.

It's really warm in my room tonight. The window's open, but there's not a breath of air. I read a bit, write down some of Great-grandfather's story in my journal, and throw off the quilt before I go to sleep.

PETERBOROUGH, ONTARIO, CANADA

June 1907

Skivvy

I can smell the storm brewing. Heat hangs in the air, lingering like dust mites in the rooms as if they haven't been cleaned. Where I sleep near the roof, it's as hot as the big kitchen stove.

It's early when I go out to clean the henhouse, feed the birds, and gather the eggs. The hens cluck and flap their wings, running round in circles as if trying to tell me something. Perspiration trickles down the back of my dress. I'd twisted my hair up this morning to keep it off my neck. If only there was a breeze, just for a minute. What wouldn't I give to lie in the grass under the apple tree? The leaves on the big maple hang so still, they look as if they've been painted on.

Back in the scullery I wash the eggs, hating the sight of the specks of blood on the eggshells more than usual.

I'd better watch myself today; heat makes adults irritable, quicker to find fault.

Mrs. Dunn is keeping to her room with a nervous headache. That means extra trips up and down stairs with cold compresses.

I sweep the dining room and hall and wipe down all the woodwork, upstairs and down, with a damp cloth. It grows warm in my hands in seconds. Just as I'm finishing, I hear Mrs. Dunn's little bell. I empty the bucket hurriedly, rinse out the cloth, hang it to dry, and go up to see what she wants. Her face is blotched red with the heat, or temper, or both. "Didn't you hear me ring, girl?" she asks, impatiently.

I'm sent on an errand to Madill's Drugstore on George Street to fetch her medicine. She orders me to hand the sealed note to Mr. Madill himself, and to come straight back. It shouldn't take any more than twenty minutes, she tells me.

Miss Alice purses her lips when she sees me getting ready to leave – there are vegetables to peel. She decides she needs lemons, and hands me a dime to buy six from Hamilton's Grocery. It's a very grand place, with food from every part of the world. This is the first time I've held a Canadian coin in my hand. Mrs. Dunn always tells me to charge everything.

I wish there was time to sit by the river and take off my boots and cool my feet in the water, but today I don't

even dare to look in the windows of the fine shops. I
know Mrs. Dunn will be lying back against her pillows
– embroidered with the words *Good Night* and *Good
Morning* – waiting for her medicine. She'll be eyeing the
hands of the big clock, under its domed-shaped glass
case, that sits on the mantel next to the photograph of
poor Mr. Dunn.

I dust the silver frame every day of the week, so I'm
getting to know his face quite well. I think he died to
get away from the sound of Mrs. Dunn's voice and the
sight of her long face, not of a heart attack at all. He's
been dead for fifteen years, but she talks as if he's about
to come in through the door for supper any minute. No
one dares to sit in his chair at mealtimes.

There's hardly anyone out on the streets now, and
I'm out of breath because I ran almost all the way back
along the dusty boardwalk. Mr. Madill warned me to get
home because we're in for a big electric storm. I get back
indoors just before the first peal of thunder.

Miss Alice sends me up with beef tea for Mrs. Dunn.
I put her medicine on the tray, bracing myself for a scold-
ing, but a big clap of thunder silences her, and I excuse
myself and go downstairs. Miss Alice points to a heap of
potatoes that I'm to peel for tonight's supper. When I've
finished those, there's rhubarb to prepare for pies.

Miss Alice goes upstairs to sit with her sister and I do
my chores to the sound of the scullery windows rattling.

I count ten lightning strikes before the rain begins to come down in great big welcome drops, barrels and buckets of it.

It's the first night I've waited at table that Mrs. Dunn hasn't come down to supper, which is served punctually at six o'clock. My place is by the sideboard, where I've carried the dishes of food. Miss Alice is always the last to enter, her round face flushed, her hands smelling of flour and cinnamon. Then Mrs. Dunn says, "At last you are here, sister," as if she's been out walking instead of cooking and baking. We lower our heads, while Mrs. Dunn says grace.

Mrs. Selena Dunn is not at all like Miss Alice, who loves to cook and eat and is as plump as a pudding. Mrs. Dunn is pale, thin, and stern, and her opinion is law. She will not be interrupted or contradicted. They refer to each other as sister, but you can tell who is in charge. Mrs. Dunn sits at the head of the table. Miss Alice sits beside her sister, and Mr. George Bell, who works at the barber-shop on Simcoe Street, sits between Miss Alice and Miss Emma Bartley. Mr. Bell's hair is very shiny and black – there is always a ring of grease on his pillowcase, which has to be boiled extra long to remove the stain. Miss Bartley, who shares a room with Mrs. Minnie Pratt, works as an alteration hand at Turnbull's Department Store. Mrs. Dunn has instructed me to tell her if I find any pins on the floor of their room because she says, "I will not permit my premises to be used for business purposes."

Miss Emma is very pretty, with long golden cork-screw curls. Mr. Bell is most attentive to her. One evening, when Miss Emma spilt some water on her skirt, Mr. Bell helped her mop it up with his napkin, and then they both blushed crimson when Mrs. Dunn told me to fetch a dry napkin.

My favorite boarder is Mrs. Minnie Pratt. She is a widow; her husband died only three weeks after their wedding day. He was killed in a hunting accident at Fenelon Falls. A wedding picture is on a dresser in her room. He looks such a happy young man. Mrs. Pratt moved here to take a business course at Peterborough Business College – that's the big building on the corner of Hunter and George Streets.

Mrs. Florence, who comes in on Mondays to do the heavy laundry, mutters about the boarders as we scrub away. She doesn't expect a reply, not that I've enough breath to speak after carrying steaming pots of water into the scullery and pulling sheets through the wringer, but I do enjoy hearing her gossip.

Mrs. Pratt is a very new widow, only nineteen years old. Sometimes I see her eyes fill with tears at the table, for no reason at all, and then she wipes them with an embroidered handkerchief. She sits on the other side, between Mr. Don Mason and Mr. Andrew Norman, who thinks he's grander than the other boarders. He works in a bank, where he wears a black suit, with a gold watch and chain on his waistcoat.

Mr. Mason is a driver for Stock's Bread. Stock's delivers all over the city in smart black horse-drawn carriages. I wonder if Mr. Mason guesses that Miss Alice often serves day-old bread to the boarders for supper. She showed me how to plunge the loaf in cold water, then squeeze it out and put it in a baking tin and bake it again in a hot oven.

Every time I bring the basket of warm bread to the table, Mrs. Dunn repeats the exact same words: "Ah, fresh baking. How Mr. Dunn used to enjoy a good fresh loaf." One night I swear I saw Mr. Mason turn to Mrs. Pratt and wink. I wouldn't be at all surprised if he asks her to go and hear him play at one of the summer band concerts. He's a trumpeter for the Peterborough City Band.

Because of the storm giving her a migraine, I carry Mrs. Dunn's supper upstairs to her tonight.

After Miss Alice finishes saying grace, I place the big platter of cold glazed ham in front of her to serve. She carves thick slices, giving more to the gentlemen than the ladies. I pass the plates round, then put dishes of potato salad and jellied salad in the center of the table.

Miss Alice serves up my dinner before she leaves the kitchen, deciding what I'm to eat. My plate is kept warm for me on the oven rack, or, on a hot night, cool in the larder. After I've brought in the pudding – dessert, as it's called in Canada – I clear away the dirty plates and cutlery and put them to soak before I sit down to my own supper in the kitchen. Sometimes I'm almost too tired to eat, knowing I've still got all the dishes to wash and wipe, the kitchen to sweep and mop, and the breakfast table to set. Most nights there are boots to brush and polish.

I refill the water glasses, holding the heavy pitcher with both hands so as not to spill a drop.

Mr. Norman smiles toothily at Miss Alice, who sits opposite. "A delicious repast, madam, perfect for such a sultry evening."

As I go about my duties, the boarders are full of stories about the storm. Mr. Mason says he'd heard that a horse left sheltering under a tree was electrocuted and one of the newly put in telephone poles on our own street, Water Street, was struck. Minnie Pratt gives a little scream and Mr. Mason pats her hand to calm her. She's what Miss Dodds would call high-strung. Mr. Bell says one of his customers told him that many people took shelter in basements and closets.

"For once I was glad the alteration hands work below the main floor at Turnbull's," Miss Bartley says. "I don't mind admitting we were all afraid."

"Almost an inch of rain fell today," Mr. Mason says. "That must be some kind of record. I had a real job trying to settle my horse down. I was late with my deliveries, I'm afraid." He always has something of interest to contribute.

"We are ready for dessert, girl. What are you waiting for?" Miss Alice reminds me sharply. "Clear the plates and bring in the pies." I'd been standing there, listening to all of them, longing to join in and tell how I'd run away from the black clouds, my boots clattering on the wooden boardwalk . . . about how the rain drummed on the roof of my little room and sounded louder than thunder. I'd quite forgotten my responsibilities.

My chores done, I'm free to go to bed. Too tired to sleep, I stand staring out into the darkness. The howling of the wind reaches into the corners of the attic; black rain streams endlessly down the glass. *Am I the only person in the world still awake?*

HALIFAX, NOVA SCOTIA, CANADA

July 2005

Thief

I'm suddenly wide-awake. I've been dreaming of the girl again. The rain on my window is as loud as hailstones, and peals of thunder follow a flash of lightning that brightens the whole room. I love looking out at a storm. The wind sings, sounding almost human.

It's her – the girl in my dream. She's watching the storm too. Her arms hug her skinny body. I slide out of bed and stand beside her.

Gran bursts in, holding a flashlight. "Good gracious, Katie, what are you doing out of bed?" *Honestly, what kind of question is that?* Gran shuts the window, and flings her arm around me. "Fierce, isn't it? I just wanted to check that you're alright. I'm concerned about the wiring up here. We've had it looked at, but. . . ."

"You worry, right? I bet it's working okay." I switch on the light. "There, it's fine." I climb back into bed.

"Good night, Katie. Sleep well."

"Night."

Gran leaves, and I turn off the light. I shut my eyes, wanting to get back into my dream. The wind's gone quiet and I can barely hear the rain.

Someone's in the room; I feel it. I'm not dreaming, at least I don't think I am. I wait a few minutes before I get up and sit on the edge of my bed.

She's here; she never left. The girl is in the alcove, crouched on the floor by Aunt Millicent's trunk. Her legs are tucked under her shapeless dress; her feet are bare.

"Hello," I whisper, "I thought I heard you humming a little while ago."

"The storm was so loud I didn't think anyone would hear. I like to sing; it reminds me of Helen. I talk to her sometimes, when I'm by myself."

"Who is Helen?" *We're actually having a conversation. Will I remember it in the morning?*

"She's someone I knew long ago. We pretended we were sisters. Helen was a skivvy, but she was aiming for something better. She gave me a picture postcard and a flower. I'm going to keep them forever. We used to sing and dance like this: Ta-ra-ra Boom-de-ay." The girl gets to her feet, and holds out her hands to me.

I take them, and we sort of polka around the room. She stops suddenly, drops my hands, shivers, and sits down on the end of my bed. I pull the quilt round her shoulders. "Helen died a long time ago. She was my mother."

"I'm awfully sorry. My mother's dead too. Please, what is a skivvy?"

"It's what I am, bottom of the heap. First up in the morning and last to bed. I work all day long for my keep. When I'm fourteen, I'll get paid wages."

"Yes, but who are you?"

"I'm a Home girl. A pair of hands to do the chores, that's all."

"That's amazing . . . I mean, are you okay? Do they treat you alright?"

"Yes and no. I've a roof over my head, and they don't beat me. I get enough to eat, and that's something to be thankful for. It's the first time in my life I've had a room to myself and there's space to stand up in it, though it's no bigger than a broom closet. There are hooks on the wall for my things, and sheets on the bed. I've a window to look out of, and I talk to the rock doves when I'm lonely and bursting to speak to someone. But that's not what I came for. It's not what they promised."

"What did they promise?" I reach out my hand to her. "Who promised?"

There is an electric feeling in the room, as though the air has been disturbed. She's gone.

It's almost light. This is the first time that I dreamt I spoke to the girl, such a sad girl. I want her to be real and I want to be her friend.

She talks to her mother too. I always thought I was the only one in the world who did that.

The quilt is back on my bed, as though I had never moved it.

I wake feeling as cranky as if I'd stayed up all night. It's just after ten. I go downstairs, drink some juice, and crash out on the deck. I may as well try to get a tan.

"Katie, did you remember to put on sunscreen?" Gran's voice jars me.

"Mmm?" I must have dozed off for a minute.

"Sunscreen, and grab a sweater please. We're going for a drive."

What is she talking about? I just want to be left alone.

"Come along, Katie. Have you forgotten we're going to Peggy's Cove? The day will be over if we don't get started soon. And yes, you do need a sweater because you know how windy it gets up there." Gran would tell me to bring a sweater even if we were going to the Caribbean.

Ten minutes later, we're heading out of the city.

"Normally I wouldn't make this trip at the height of the season," Gran announces. *So how come we're going then?* "We'll try not to let the tourist buses spoil our day.

I hope we can find a place to park." Gran is acting like this was my idea.

I shouldn't have skipped breakfast, I'm famished. Naturally there's a twenty-minute lineup for lunch at the Sou'Wester. They seat us eventually and we order seafood chowder and corn bread.

"I think it's time you and I had a talk, Katie," Gran says, as she butters her bread. *We talk all day – what now?*

"I don't want to pry, but are you worried about anything? Won't you tell me about it? Perhaps I can help. Grandfather and I want you to have a happy time with us." *Is that why we drove two hours out here? We could have had this conversation at the house.*

"Excuse me, but I have to find the washroom." *What is wrong with her? What right do adults have to be so intrusive? It's like they ask us about school all the time, so who's going to admit that things aren't perfect?*

I wash my face with cold water, comb my hair, and go back to the table.

The chowder's cold. I put my spoon down and say, "The thing is, Gran, I've got a lot of stuff happening in my life right now and I need to work it out, okay?" I was going to leave it at that, but the words sort of spill out. "If you must know, I am not thrilled about having to share the house, or my father, with Step. Where do I fit into this cozy threesome? I'm supposed to be happy about a baby? Some people might think it isn't a big deal to feel like an outsider in your own home, but it is to me — it's a very big deal."

I'm not trying to be rude, but Gran asked me, and it's the truth. *I wish that for just one day I could have my mom back.*

We sit in this huge silence and I'm finding it hard to swallow. After what seems like hours, Gran says, "Thank you for telling me, Katie."

"I'll work it out, okay, Gran?" Amazingly she doesn't say any more. We don't have dessert, though there's gingerbread and ice cream on the menu, which Gran says is her favorite.

We get through the afternoon somehow. I send off postcards of the lighthouse to Mel and Angie. We don't say much on the way home.

While Gran waters the garden, I decide to make her some gingerbread. I line up the ingredients on the counter, saying the name of each one out loud, the way I did the first time Mom taught me the recipe — the way I still do it every single time I bake.

Grandfather eats three cookies the minute they come out of the oven, and Gran says, "Perfect." She suggests I bring a few for Miss Macready when I visit her tomorrow.

I go upstairs early and read over my audition speech for *The Secret Garden*. I want to play Mary Lennox so badly. Not just because it's a terrific and challenging role, but because she finds her own way to become a part of her new family.

The scene I've chosen is where she has a huge fight with Colin, and shows him there's nothing wrong with his back.

The sound of crying wakes me. It's so loud I'm surprised Gran hasn't woken up too. *Is it me, crying in my sleep?* I was on the edge of tears all afternoon.

I get through the days, and they're okay, but at night I feel as if I'm taking part in a story, and I can hardly wait to find out what's going to happen next.

There is someone else in the room. The "sad girl" huddles in her usual place, crouched beside the trunk. She's trying hard not to cry, but now and again I hear a great gulping sob. It makes me want to cry too, to comfort her even before I know what's wrong. I slide out of bed and sit down cross-legged on the floor, facing her.

"Please tell me why you're upset. I won't tell anyone; you can trust me," I whisper, afraid she'll disappear.

"It's not fair, it's not fair," she sobs.

"What isn't fair?" I ask, willing her to stay, not taking my eyes off her.

"Miss Alice searched my room, turned it all upside down. Mrs. Dunn must have put her up to it. They had no right. . . ."

"Of course, they didn't. It's against the law to treat you like that."

"What law? I've heard of no law for orphans. They can accuse Home children of stealing without proof, if they've a mind to, and there's no one to speak up for us." She wipes her eyes.

I don't know how to help, except to listen and tell her I'm on her side. "Why did they accuse you?"

"It's all that Mr. Norman's fault. He's been eyeing me for weeks. Sometimes when I'm handing round the plates at table, he brushes my arm, or he comes out of his room when he hears me on the landing. It's narrow even for one person up there. It gives him an excuse to stand close to me, pretending he just happened to be there at the same time.

"I've grown out of both my work dresses. They're too tight, and too short. I've moved the buttons and let down the hems as much as they'll go. That's the best I can do. I've been here more than a year – I've grown. I'll be thirteen in two months, and I'm supposed to be provided with my board and keep. By rights Mrs. Dunn should get me another dress, but I don't like to ask her.

"The Sunday school picnic was on Saturday. St. John's Anglican Church is where Mrs. Dunn and Miss Alice worship, and where I attend Sunday school. I was allowed to go, as long as my chores were done. I polished the silver, washed the scullery floor and the new gray linoleum in the kitchen, and blackleaded the stove. Then I changed into my Sunday dress. It's dark blue flannel and still fits me because they made it to fit big back in London.

"I was told to return from the outing in plenty of time to help Miss Alice with Saturday night supper. Finally I was free to leave. I did feel happy, being out in the fresh air amongst the trees and flowers, with a whole afternoon ahead to enjoy myself with other girls my age.

"I'd never been on a picnic before. Miss Farrell, our Sunday school teacher, took us to Jackson Park, and we settled under the shade of some sycamore trees. We spread out a big white linen cloth, and laid out the food. I added Miss Alice's famous corn bread to the feast as my contribution. There were layer cakes, tea biscuits, jam tarts, and a lemon sponge. We had hard-boiled eggs and ham sandwiches and two cold roast chickens. More food than I'd ever seen at one meal.

"I have enough to eat, but I don't get everything the same as the boarders. Not that I'm complaining; it's a lot better than I ever had back home. Miss Farrell brought lemonade for everyone and candied fruits as a special treat.

"After we'd cleared away and scattered crumbs for the birds, we played games like I spy and hide-and-go-seek and jump rope. Then Miss Farrell gathered us in a circle and talked about children less fortunate than ourselves. The class agreed to give all the leftover food to the

Children's Aid shelter at the north end of Water Street. The teacher said I might deliver it on my way home, as I live on Water Street too. She said that I was never to forget that once I was one of those unfortunate children, and wasn't I lucky to have found a good home? They like to remind you where you come from . . . make sure that you're properly grateful.

"It got hotter and hotter, and Miss Farrell said we could walk quietly in the park for an hour before it was time to leave. She sat down on a blanket to rest, and the others went off in small groups.

"I don't have a special friend because of being a Home girl and working as a skivvy, but Sadie Johnston and Millie Hughes asked if I wanted to go to the creek, below Bonaccord Street, with them. Millie's big brother had seen two blue herons there that week. A heron was still there, standing on one leg, motionless as a stone, almost as though he had been carved out of air. He never moved, not even when we took off our shoes and stockings to go into the water to cool off.

"We waded in, lifting our skirts up to our knees. Suddenly Millie screamed, pointing towards the bushes. The heron, startled, rose up and flew away.

"'A man, there's a man looking at us!' she yelled. We grabbed hold of each other's hands and scrambled back to the bank, picking up our things and running till we were breathless. We dried our feet as best as we could with our petticoats, hoping Miss Farrell wouldn't notice. But Millie was in hysterics, crying about a man with glaring eyes. Miss Farrell tried to comfort her, then looking directly at me, she said coldly, 'I will not enquire whose idea it was to go to the creek, but I hope you have all learned a lesson, and will behave in a more seemly manner in future.'

"We walked back to the church, where the mothers were waiting to pick up their daughters. I carried the remains of the picnic to the children's shelter, and was back in time to help Miss Alice. I thanked her again for the corn bread and she set me to scraping carrots and new potatoes.

"After supper that night, when Miss Alice had put the leftover roast in the pantry, she reminded me to scour the sink in the scullery and then went upstairs to the parlor. I was sweeping the floor when Mr. Norman came in. He was holding a small box in his hand. 'I thought you might like a chocolate,' he said, and offered me a gold-wrapped sweet. 'It must have been most refreshing, paddling in the creek this afternoon, the water cool on your bare feet and legs.' He stared at me and I remembered how we'd waded into that lovely water, our skirts held too high. And then I knew he was the man who'd seen us – the man in the bushes! He looked so pleased with himself, I wanted to sweep him out of the room.

"'Yes, sir, it was . . . very refreshing, and no, sir, I don't want a chocolate. I had sufficient to eat at the picnic. If you'll excuse me, I have to finish my work now.'

"'Some other time, perhaps,' he said, and stood, watching me, like a cat waiting to pounce.

"At that moment, Mrs. Dunn came into kitchen. 'Do you require anything, Mr. Norman?' she asked. Then, harshly to me, 'You are late with my tea, girl. Bring the tray upstairs as soon as it's ready.'

"I lifted the steaming kettle off the hob and heard Mr. Norman say, as they left the room, 'I was looking for you, dear madam, to give you a small gift. Today I was informed that I am being transferred to the Toronto branch of the bank, and sadly I shall be leaving your delightful establishment at the end of the week.'

"It was as if someone had lifted a great weight from me."

"He was trying to bribe you with chocolate, so that you wouldn't say anything, wasn't he?" I ask.

She stops crying now and says, "I thought I was safe from him. He'd be gone in a few days. I vowed not to go anywhere near him, to keep out of his way as much as I could. A few days later, I was putting the clean towels away in the closet upstairs. I had to stand on tiptoe because it's hard for me to reach the top shelf. I felt two hands on my waist and then they slid along my arms. When I felt his mouth on the side of my neck, I ducked my head and kicked his shins with all my strength.

" 'Don't you ever touch me again,' I said, and ran downstairs and got my pail and brush and scrubbed the front steps until my wrists ached. My dress had a tear under the arm where I'd pulled away from him, but I could bear anything, knowing he'd be gone by Saturday."

"Why didn't you tell someone?"

"Who'd believe me? What could I say? That he followed us at the picnic, that he offered me a sweet, that he helped me put the towels away? Who'd even listen? The only person I ever met who'd speak up for me is far away, slaving on a farm, I expect. I miss him."

I take her hand and hold it, feeling how rough her skin is compared to mine.

"Tell me what happened then," I say.

"After lunch the next day, Mrs. Dunn sent for me. I went upstairs wondering what I had done to upset her. I'd cobbled my dress together somehow, so it wasn't that. I'd given the parlor a good turnout, waxed and polished the furniture, including the piano, which is never touched because Mr. Dunn used to play it, and which is covered with a lace cloth. A big brass pot of ferns stands in the middle of the piano and I'd made sure it gleamed. I'd dusted the fire screen, carefully brushing the embroidered peacock on it with the wool duster. The china candlesticks, decorated with tiny rosebuds, had been washed in warm soapy water and dried with a soft cloth. After I'd neatened the cushions on the blue damask sofa and straightened the blue silk scarf that lay over the back of it, I'd wiped the big mirror and both windows with vinegar and water, until they squeaked.

"I knocked on the door, even though it was open. Mrs. Dunn was at her desk doing her accounts. She blotted the page she'd been writing on before walking over to one of the high-backed blue fireside chairs. As soon as she was seated, I carried the matching footstool over to her and waited for instructions. She looked as if she had one of her nervous headaches.

"'I have received a complaint regarding your conduct from one of my boarders.' I braced myself for the lecture that was sure to follow. I knew what was coming, or thought I did. Mr. Norman must have told her that I'd been disrespectful.

"'Mr. Norman tells me that this morning he left his watch chain on his washstand, and when he returned at lunchtime, the chain was missing. You are the only person to have entered Mr. Norman's room today. What have you done with it?'

"'I have done nothing because I never took it. What use would a watch chain be to me, ma'am?' I said.

"Before Mrs. Dunn had time to answer, Miss Alice came in and said, 'Nothing, sister.' What did she mean by 'nothing'? I opened my mouth to speak, but Mrs. Dunn stopped me.

"'I do not wish to hear another word from you, impudent girl. You will accompany Miss Alice to the scullery and she will search your person for the missing article.'

"I swore that I had not taken anything; told them that I'd tidied Mr. Norman's room as usual and left a clean towel for him on the washstand. I said he had not left the watch chain in his room – why would he, when he always wore the watch to work? 'If he says I'm a thief, then he is a liar,' I said boldly.

"Mrs. Dunn slapped me then for speaking out of turn and told me that Mr. Norman was taking his watch to the watch repairer to be cleaned. Miss Alice grabbed my arm and pushed me out of the room. Downstairs, she stood over me, while I removed my shoes and dress and apron and shook out my petticoat. Then she hustled me back upstairs. I pulled away from her and said, 'I am not a thief, Mrs. Dunn, as you well know. You can count the apples in the fruit bowl, the spoons in the sideboard, and never find one missing. I don't take what doesn't belong to me. Perhaps Mr. Norman misplaced the chain.'

"The sisters looked at each other, and without another word I marched out and into Mr. Norman's room. They followed me and watched from the doorway.

I looked in the dresser, inside the wardrobe, and under the bed. When I stripped the bed, I found the chain lying below the undersheet, on top of the wool mattress. 'Here it is,' I said, and handed it to Miss Alice.

"Mrs. Dunn ordered me to make up the room again, and then to brew her tea and bring it up to her."

"You mean, they didn't apologize to you?" I ask.

"Not a word. I made up the bed, punching the bolster and wishing it was his face, then went downstairs to make the tea. When I brought up the tray, Mrs. Dunn told me to pour her a cup. I handed it to her, expecting a kind word after all that had happened. 'Do you remember what I told you, when you came here a year ago?' she asked me.

"Luckily she didn't wait for an answer, because I couldn't have remembered a word just then.

"'I spoke to you about the importance of having an unblemished character. You are fortunate that I am not dismissing you on the spot, and returning you to Dr. Barnardo's Home without a character reference.'

"'But I didn't do anything. Mr. Norman made it all up for spite.'

"'Even the hint of a complaint against a servant is enough to destroy her character. Why would a gentleman like Mr. Norman bother with a girl like you? Unless,' she cleared her throat, 'you have provoked him in some way. If ever I have cause to speak to you on such a matter again, you will be dismissed instantly. I will make sure that no respectable establishment will ever hire you. Now turn around. I am not pleased with your appearance. Tomorrow you will be provided with material to make yourself a dress that covers you decently. Go and finish your work.'

"That night, when I went upstairs to my room, I saw what Miss Alice had done – what she meant when she'd said 'nothing.' My ribbon was lying crumpled on the floor and worse, so was the picture postcard that Helen had given me. My bed had been stripped down to the mattress, and not made up again. I tried not to cry. I was so tired and sad. The worst I'd ever felt since Helen died and I didn't shed tears then.

"Why can't they call me by my name? It's always 'you' or 'girl.' I'm treated like a piece of dirt off the street. I want a place where I'm wanted; I want a family, the way they promised us."

"I'm Katie, won't you please tell me your name?" I reach for her hand, but she vanishes, goes away again to that other world of hers, where I can't follow. Before I fall asleep, I hear her whisper, "My name is Lillie."

Lily? That's Colin's mother's name. I'm so mixed up, all the stories jumble in my head and I can't sort them out. Next morning I wake up still on the floor, and my hand is on the lid of the trunk, touching the letter *L*.

PETERBOROUGH, ONTARIO, CANADA

July 1909

Gypsy

The window is open, and the sweet smell of the late-evening breeze from the lake and the garden creeps into the attic. It's dark, my candle has burned right down, and I'm not due for another one until Friday, but I don't care.

I have so much to tell you, Helen, I hardly know where to begin. My thoughts are tangled like a skein of wool that needs unraveling.

I want to tell you every single thing that's happened this week. I want to write you a letter, and roll it up and tie it to the leg of the little rock dove that's cooing on the roof, and send it up to you in Heaven. If only I could. But I know you're up there, listening to me.

It all started on Tuesday – ironing day. While I was waiting for the flatirons to heat, I scoured the kitchen garden for slugs. They are awfully bad this year. Miss Alice looks at me accusingly when I bring in the vegetables, as if it were me who'd nibbled holes in the lettuce, instead of the slugs. That day I knelt down and sprinkled each of their slimy little bodies with salt. When they stopped writhing, I dropped them into my pail. It turned my stomach having to do that.

A voice said, "If you circle the vegetables with crushed eggshells, it keeps the slugs away." A girl about my age looked down at me. I stood up and thanked her. We were almost the same height. Her glossy black hair fell in two thick braids, almost to her waist. I felt drab beside her in my patched blue work dress. She looked so colorful in her red skirt, white blouse, and black bodice, richly embroidered with beads and flowers. I recognized her as one of the Gypsies who'd been camping at South End Park, waiting for their menfolk to be released from jail. The whole town had been abuzz about them. They caused more stir and gossip than the circus. I heard they were moving on to Ottawa, now that the men have been freed. Mrs. Dunn had me counting the washing every time I took it off the line because some of the neighbors had missed sheets and pillowcases and blamed the Gypsies.

The girl smiled at me, showing sparkling white teeth. She pulled a wooden peg from the woven bag she was carrying and asked me if we needed some clothes-pegs.

I'd already taken down the clothes and rolled them up in the laundry basket, which I'd carried inside for ironing. I shook my head.

When she offered to tell my fortune, I said, "I have no money, but I'll let you have my lunch in exchange." I ran in and got the bread and cold bacon left out for me from the boarders' breakfast. When I returned, the girl had settled herself against the young maple tree, her eyes shut tight against the midmorning sun.

Miss Alice and Mrs. Dunn wouldn't be home for a while yet. They'd gone to a luncheon meeting at the Women's Christian Temperance Union.

The girl stuffed the food into her mouth and asked me where I came from. I told her I'd crossed the ocean two years ago, from England.

She said, "You could be one of us, with your dark hair and skin. Hold out your left hand." She bent over my palm, and her necklace of silver coins glittered and jangled above my wrist.

"I see a journey," she said. Well, I'm not a fool; I had mentioned that already. I hoped she could do better than that in exchange for my lunch.

"Do you mean another journey?" I asked her.

She put her forefinger across my lips. "I see more travel. There is a child you guard who is not yours." She held up my hand, and looked at the lines on the side of my palm. "But I see three more – your own. A fair-haired man is waiting for you. He waits without knowing how to find you, or where. He will love you forever and you him." She tossed her braids back over her shoulders, and said, "It is a good fortune." She licked the bacon fat off her fingers and stood up. "Why stay here? Come and travel with us."

Would you have gone, Helen? *Why not?* I thought. For a moment I dreamed of what it would mean – to be part of a band of wanderers, to make my home in a wagon, to wear rings on my fingers, and silver hoops in my ears. At night, around the campfire, there would be music and dancing. Mrs. Florence said she had seen the Gypsies in their campground.

I was tempted to say yes, but I could never really be one of them. I would always be an outsider wanting to stay in one place and make a home. I thanked the girl and watched her go, her red skirt swinging from side to side as she moved gracefully through the grass on her slender bare feet. She stopped at the gate, turned, and waved to me in farewell. I waved back, but dropped my arm quickly at the sight of the sisters returning to the house.

"How dare you let a Gypsy into the yard. They are all thieves! What did she want?" Mrs. Dunn said, glaring at me. I don't know what got into me, but I told her that the girl had asked me to go along with her.

I thought Mrs. Dunn would explode; her face turned as red as a beet. "No doubt she recognized you as kin," she said, and walked away in a rage, leaving Miss Alice and me to follow her indoors.

Miss Alice said, "You'll not leave this kitchen until you've finished the ironing, and when that's done, I want the stove cleaned out."

It was three o'clock before I'd finished and I was dizzy with hunger, not having eaten my lunch. Miss Alice decided she needed oranges to make a fruit salad and sent me out for a dozen. She gave me forty cents, and told me not to lose the change.

The market was bustling and there were several people waiting in front of me. I closed my fingers tightly around the nickel, when the Italian fruit-seller gave me my change, and hurried away.

On my way back, I had to pass by the Oriental Hotel. It's said to be the grandest of all the hotels in Peterborough, with private bathrooms and electric lights in all the rooms. A smartly uniformed nursemaid waited on the steps, trying to restrain a little girl, not much more than a baby, who was hugging a ball and jumping up and down. The nursemaid turned her head to speak to the doorman, letting go of the child's hand, and in that instant, the little girl dropped her ball and ran after it.

It all happened in seconds. The red ball bounced into the gutter and rolled between the hooves of a pair of black horses pulling an elegant carriage, just coming to a stop in front of the hotel. I heard the coachman shout *whoa* as I threw myself off the boardwalk, my oranges flying in all directions, to grab the child away from the stamping hooves.

The nursemaid was screaming hysterically; the little girl crying, "Ball, ball." I'd ripped my apron and scraped my elbow, but the child was safe. By this time, her mother had jumped out of the carriage and onto the boardwalk. She took the little one into her arms and was crying over her, holding her tightly against her silk gown.

I gathered up my oranges, wiped the dust off them, picked up the ball, and gave it to the little girl before the nursemaid took her inside.

Her mother turned to me, put her hand gently on my arm, and said, "I don't know how to thank you. You saved my little girl from a terrible accident! Your mother will be so worried about you, anxious that you have been delayed on your errand. Driver, please take this young lady home." She gave me her calling card and said she would be staying in the hotel for a few more days. Then she pressed five whole dollars into my hand, as a reward for my courage.

"There is no need for this, ma'am. I'm happy the little girl came to no harm," I said, but she insisted I take it. The driver opened the door, asked where I lived, and drove me back. Luckily, I was not too late returning from my errand.

When I gave Miss Alice her change, a blister had formed in my palm from holding the nickel so tightly. I explained that I'd had a fall, that there'd been an accident, but she wasn't interested. She just sent me to change my apron, wash my hands, get the oranges peeled and sliced, and the table set for supper.

After I'd made the last pot of tea for the evening, Miss Alice gave me a list of chores to do for the following day. She and Mrs. Dunn planned to leave for Bethel next morning to visit some cousins on their farm outside Peterborough, and would not be back until after supper. I was told to rinse the tea leaves that night and sprinkle them on the parlor carpet, so I could give the carpet a thorough brushing in the morning. Mrs. Dunn had complained the dust in the room was intolerable. I was not to forget to scrub the kitchen and scullery and put a cupful of vinegar in the last rinse, to keep the ants away.

For supper, I was to serve the remains of the cold roast beef, make potato cakes, hot biscuits, and a mixed salad. Then I was to stew apples and serve them with a vanilla sauce for dessert. If I had time on my hands, as I was bound to, the scullery windows were a disgrace, and should have been washed without my having to be told.

Before they left in the morning, Mrs. Dunn, who had not spoken to me since she'd seen the Gypsy, reminded me that while a mistress was away, her orders must be carried out as if she were there. "I shall do my best, ma'am," I answered, scarcely able to contain my excitement.

I set to work, flying from room to room. There was no lunch to prepare, as the present boarders did not normally return until the evening meal.

Do you remember how you and I had days out, Helen? I've never forgotten, and I've often dreamed of another such day. I stayed awake almost the whole night planning what I was going to do with the hour or two I'd have free before I needed to prepare supper.

By noon the floors gleamed, the woodwork shone, and the carpets were brushed. I went upstairs to wash, put on my Sunday dress, and tie up my hair with a Sunday ribbon before strolling out of the house, swinging my hips the way the Gypsy girl had done. Then, as I got near to the Bank of Toronto, I walked more sedately. I had to take a deep breath to give myself courage (as I had never been in a bank before), went in, approached the counter, and asked the clerk to please give me change for a five-dollar bill.

My next stop was at the stationery shop for paper, envelopes, and a pencil. That took care of almost a whole dollar.

I had heard the girls in school talk about Fowler's Ice-cream Parlor. It was where their mothers and aunts took them for a special treat. Today was my special treat. I was having a day out. It would have been nice to tell the girls that I'd been to the ice-cream parlor too, but I'd be fourteen in two months' time and had finished with school. Mrs. Dunn had permitted me to go for only a few weeks because she said I was needed at the house due to her ill health. I didn't mind too much; I'd learnt to read and write at the Girls' Village Home school in Essex.

When the waitress, looking smart in her black dress and lace apron and cap, handed me the menu, I was too nervous to speak and just pointed to the first item without reading it. The young lady brought me two scoops of vanilla ice cream in a silver dish. There was a wafer, shaped like a three cornered hat, and a glacé cherry on top of each scoop. Nothing in my whole life had ever tasted better than that first delicious bite, Helen. There was a glass of water to drink, too.

After I'd finished, I took a piece of my new stationery and composed a letter right there in the ice-cream parlor.

Wednesday, July 7, 1909

Dear Madam,
I hope your little girl has suffered no ill effects from her fright yesterday. It was very kind of you to send me home in a carriage and to reward me so generously. It is the first time that I have had money of my very own.

My name is Lillie Bridges. I will be fourteen years old in September. I have been working as a domestic at Mrs. Dunn's boarding house, on Water Street, for the last two years.

I arrived in Canada in 1907, one of a group of Barnardo orphans. I used to help take care of the younger children in the Girls' Village Home in Essex, England. I like looking after little ones very much.

Please forgive me for troubling you, but perhaps you might hear of a situation where a family has need of an honest hardworking girl.

   I remain,
   Yours respectfully,
   Lillie Bridges

Reading the letter through again, I wished my penmanship was more elegant. Ever since I was a small girl, there'd been reprimands for writing with my left hand. They'd forced me to use my right, and now I don't write well with either.

I got up from the table, left a five-cent tip, and walked over to the Oriental Hotel to deliver my envelope. The doorman touched his cap. He recognized me and promised to hand over my letter himself.

I'm too old to skip, and girls don't whistle, so instead, I sang under my breath all the way back to the boarding house.

When the sisters came in, complaining about the long tiring drive, I'd finished scrubbing the pots, swept up, set out the breakfast things, and had the kettle boiling for tea. I carried the tray up to the parlor, poured the tea, and asked Mrs. Dunn if there was anything else she required.

She said, "I have something to say to you. My cousins, Mr. and Mrs. Angus Bird, need a girl for both outside and indoor work on the farm. They are prepared to give you a trial. I have had a word with Matron at Dr. Barnardo's Home for Girls. She is expecting a new shipment of girls next week. I have asked her to pick me out a ten-year-old. I feel that you would do better away from the temptations of the city. However, I have given a fair account of you, despite certain incidents. You may stay for another week or two, and help settle in the new girl. She can share your room until you go the farm."

"Excuse me, ma'am," I reminded her, "I'll be fourteen in September, and am due to receive wages then."

"That will be a matter for you and my cousin, Mr. Bird, to settle. You may go. I am excessively fatigued." She rested her head against the chair and closed her eyes.

She thinks I can't see through her, Helen. She's too mean to pay me the wages she's supposed to, when I'm fourteen. She'll get four years of slavery out of a ten-year-old. Doesn't Matron understand what she's up to? As long as we're fed and don't cost the Home anything, no one cares. Not once has anyone come to see if I'm doing alright here.

The temptations of the city – did you ever hear such nonsense, Helen? I'm hardly let out of the house, except for Sunday school and errands. But Mrs. Dunn didn't refuse me a "character," so I can't complain. I'll find my way, I always have. I like the countryside. I expect I can learn to milk cows. I might even prefer them to those greedy chickens.

What if they don't like me? What if I don't suit them? Just for once it'd be nice to be asked what I want.

Next morning I was up to my elbows in soapsuds, scrubbing down the pantry shelves. I'd already finished washing and drying the china and glass, and it was ready to put back. Miss Alice was at the table, slicing onions and bits of leftover beef to grind through the mincing machine. She told me to stop what I was doing and go and answer Mrs. Dunn's bell. I dried my hands, rolled down my sleeves, and hurried upstairs. She hates to be kept waiting.

Mrs. Dunn had a visitor. It was the little girl's mother. My heart sank – had she told Mrs. Dunn about my letter? And then I thought, why shouldn't I write to her? No one had bothered to ask me if I wanted to go and work on a farm. So I bobbed a curtsy, and asked, "You rang, ma'am?" And I wished the lady good morning.

She smiled at me and said, "I've just been telling Mrs. Dunn how brave you were on Tuesday in rescuing my daughter. I have also explained that our nursemaid is indisposed, in shock, after Elisabeth's mishap, and will not be returning to Halifax with us. I do not know how I am going to manage my willful little girl on a long train trip without help.

"If you are agreeable to the arrangement, Mrs. Dunn is prepared to release you from your employment here. I hope my little Elisabeth will look up to you as she would to an older sister, and will learn by example to become a dutiful little girl. As we are leaving on Monday, I will send for you on Saturday afternoon so that you and Elisabeth may have a little time to get used to one another, prior to our journey.

"I will provide your uniform, and to start with, your salary will be five dollars per month. You may have a half day off each week, after lunch, and one full day per month. Once your little charge is asleep at night, and you have tidied the nursery and seen to her clothes, you may have the remainder of the evening to yourself. What do you say, Lillie?"

I wanted to fall on my knees and thank her, to tell her it sounded like paradise. Instead, I curtsied again and said quietly, "I would like to accept the position, ma'am, and will do my very best not to disappoint you."

"I must compliment you on Lillie's excellent manners, Mrs. Dunn. I am indebted to you." The lady picked up her gloves and bowed to Mrs. Dunn, who, for once, was all smiles, and told me to see her visitor out.

When I held open the front door for her, she smiled and said, "I think we shall all get on together quite splendidly. Good-bye until Saturday."

I didn't know whether to laugh or cry. You told me I've got to aim for something in life. Isn't this a wonderful start, Helen?

On Saturday morning, I cleaned up my room, closed the trunk, and made the bed ready for the new girl. I hoped she'd talk to my rock doves. I wrapped up a quarter for her, in a note with *Good luck* written on it, and hid it in her pillowslip, where she would find it when she changed the bedding.

When I went downstairs to say good-bye to Mrs. Dunn, I had to listen to a sermon on the duties of a good servant and watch Miss Alice nod her head in agreement. I managed to hold my tongue until the carriage arrived to fetch me, then I said, "I hope you will excuse my impertinence, Mrs. Dunn, but I have something I wish to say before I leave. You would be doing the new girl a great kindness, ma'am, if you and Miss Alice were to call her by her own name." And then I walked out, ready to begin my new life.

The Gypsy said I would be looking after a child who

was not my own. That part has come true. Will I also meet the fair-haired man who is waiting for me?

If Maria was here, instead of back at the Girls' Village Home in Essex, how she'd tease me! Just the way she did on the boat for talking to a boy. He had fair hair. I liked him and I wish we'd exchanged names. He called me Flower. I hope he found the kind family they promised us. You never know, we might meet again someday. Anything can happen, Helen. Look at the way my life has changed!

HALIFAX, NOVA SCOTIA, CANADA

July 2005

Flower

Tomorrow I visit Miss Macready. I want to find out if she talks to the ghost of the sea captain, the way I talk to the girl who whispered her name to me.

Something wakes me up. The room is full of shadows and Lillie emerges from them. She seems different tonight, kind of hesitant, as if she's here for the first time. She runs her hand over the furniture, touches the jug and basin on the chest, then stands by the window and looks out onto the garden. I say her name softly: "Lillie?" She doesn't answer. Lillie's far away, in a dream of her own. I don't think she can hear me. I hope she's not feeling sad tonight. She doesn't stay.

★

The nursing home looks better than it sounds. On the way here, Gran and I had a competition to see who could come up with the worst name we could think of for a seniors' home. She won with Journey's End!

The lobby is painted cream and green. There are fake trees, which only look semi-real. An old man shuffles in, hanging on tightly to the rails along the walls. There are pictures of flowers and ships, the kind you see in dentists' offices. A few old people wander through, mostly using walkers or canes. It's awfully quiet. I wish I hadn't come.

Gran asks the efficient-looking young lady at the desk where we can find Miss Macready. She checks her computer and tells us she's on the roof deck, then points us to the elevator. I've got butterflies in my stomach. *How do I bring Lillie into the conversation? Do I ask if she ever saw her too? I'd better stick to my plan of asking about her childhood.* We get off at the fifth floor.

It's really nice and relaxing up here. Pots of crimson, white, and pink geraniums stand at intervals on the waist-high brick walls. There are five or six round tables, each shaded by a green-and-white striped umbrella.

A young man wearing a white jacket wheels a trolley from table to table, offering juices, tea, or coffee to the residents, some of whom are playing cards or just napping in the afternoon sun. Gran tells him we've come to see Miss Macready, and he takes us over to her. She looks small and frail in her wheelchair, a light blue shawl draped over her shoulders.

"Your visitors are here, Miss Elisabeth, and I've brought your apple juice." He places a nonspill cup in front of her.

"It's so nice to see you again, Miss Macready. I'm Norah Carr. We met when we bought your beautiful house. This is my granddaughter Katie; she's staying with us on her vacation. Katie sleeps in the room next to your old nursery. She's been looking forward to meeting you."

I say hello and put the bunch of white and yellow daisies I picked this morning and the bag of cookies on the table in front of her.

The young man says, "I'll find a vase for your flowers, Miss Elisabeth. They will look nice in your room." She thanks him, without taking her eyes from my face. Poor Gran might as well be invisible, but when she says she'll come back for me in half an hour, Miss Macready turns to her for a moment and actually says her name. "Goodbye, Mrs. Carr."

The minute Gran leaves, Miss Macready says, "I thought she'd never go. I've waited such a long time for you." *Weird, she doesn't even know me.*

"You brought me a present — what is it?" I help her open the bag, and tell her I baked my favorite cookies for her. She fumbles for one, takes a small bite, and says,

"Not between meals, Bessie." Her shoulders shake. She's laughing and I'm afraid she might choke. I look round for the attendant.

The young man notices and comes back. "Do you need anything?" he says. Miss Macready waves him away. He adjusts the umbrella and goes off. I move my chair closer to Miss Macready.

"He's a kind young man. I'll ask him to come to my birthday party. I am going to be ninety-seven soon," she says.

"Congratulations. Did you have birthday parties when you were a little girl, Miss Macready?" I'm hoping she'll tell me about her childhood.

"Of course I did. Don't you remember how we played hide-and-seek with my guests in the garden and there was always a big cake with candles for 'dining-room tea'? Why did you go away? Why won't you take care of me the way you used to?"

Gran warned me that Miss Macready might get confused. Maybe this wasn't such a great idea.

"Hold my hand, hold Bessie's hand, the way you always did." I take her hand, which feels soft even though her knuckles are swollen. I've never met anyone this old before. Maybe she thinks I'm one of the girls who played with her in her garden. I don't know why she stares at me.

"Do you remember how I was afraid of horses?" she asks.

It's surreal out here on the rooftop. I feel as if I'm taking part in play, or a foreign movie, and I've forgotten my lines. I make a guess: "Even of your rocking horse?"

"You know I was. When Papa brought the horse upstairs to the nursery, he lifted me on and I screamed, 'I'll fall, I'll fall,' but you climbed on too and held me. You said, 'I won't let you fall, Bessie' and you sang." She half-croons in a quavering voice:

Ride a cock horse to Banbury Cross
To see my Bessie ride a white horse.
Rings on her fingers, bells on her toes,
She shall have music wherever she goes.

"Papa wanted me to learn to ride a real horse, but I never did." She gives a mischievous chuckle. "After Papa died, I told the gardener to put the horse in his shed."

"I've forgotten why you were so afraid of horses, Miss Macready."

"Now, you're teasing again. You know how I love to hear you tell me that story."

Help. I'm lost. What story? In desperation I say, "It's your turn to tell it today, Miss Bessie. We always took turns, didn't we?"

"I like it when you call me by my pet name." She starts to speak. She knows every word by heart.

"Mama and I were on holiday with Papa, who had business in Peterborough. I was not quite two years old, and I was waiting on the steps of the hotel with my nursemaid. Papa and Mama had promised to take me for a drive in the carriage. I saw it draw up, pulled by two black horses. Sometimes I still have bad dreams about them." She hangs on to her shawl and sort of shrinks inside it, as if she wants to hide.

I take hold of her hand again. "Please go on. Don't be afraid."

"I dropped my ball, my new red ball that Papa had bought for me. It rolled away, down the steps. I ran after it, ran right between the hooves of the horses. Someone screamed, and then you were there to save me. You picked me up, and said, 'No need to cry, little girl, you're safe now.'"

"I'm thirsty," she says. I hold the cup of juice to her lips. She drinks a little and then pushes the cup away, just like a small child does.

"And then you came to live with Mama and Papa and me."

"What a lovely story, Miss Bessie, but I wasn't the one who lived with you. I'm Katie – I wasn't born then."

"I remember you were like a big sister. Do you want to see my photographs?"

"I'd like that."

Her purse is beside her in her wheelchair. She can't manage to open the clasp. I help her and she pulls out two faded photos. "This one is of Mama and me, before you came to us." It is one of those old-fashioned sepia-tinted pictures — a young woman wearing a long lace dress with a high collar and a huge hat with flowers under the brim. A plump little girl about two years old, a big white bow in her hair, stands leaning against her mother's knee. On the back of the picture, it says ROY STUDIO, PETERBOROUGH, 1909.

The second photo is of the same child, a few years later, sitting on a swing. A teenage girl stands behind her, wearing a striped dress and white apron. Her hands grip the rope, as though she were about to push the swing. This one says HALIFAX, 1914. It was taken in the garden at Carpenter's Rest. It's hard to remember sometimes that the house my grandparents live in is where Miss Macready grew up. I ask her, "Who is the girl pushing the swing? What's her name?" She doesn't answer. Perhaps she thinks I ought to know.

"That was the afternoon you took me to the park. I have never forgotten that day. I had been well behaved all week, so for a treat you said you would take me for a walk in the Public Gardens. It was your afternoon off and I never liked you to go out without me.

"'Hold my hand, Bessie. Don't go running away,' you said. We went around the lake and along the stream first because I liked to watch the ducks. Then I was allowed to run over the little bridges and under the weeping willow. 'Five more minutes,' you said, 'and then home to have tea with your mama.'

"We walked back past the ornamental fountains. A soldier stood there. Many young men were in uniform at that time in Halifax. He turned around, stared at us, and said, 'Flower? It is Flower, isn't it? I've always hoped we'd meet again one day.' And you looked at each other and laughed and laughed. I didn't understand why, but I felt I'd lost you, even though you kept tight hold of my hand.

"'The boy with the smile,' you said at last. Then you and he sat down on a bench, with me between you, and the two of you talked and talked as if you'd never stop. I might just as well have stayed home for all the notice you took of me. He spoiled my treat.

"I was late for tea that day. The soldier walked us home, and shook hands with both of us. He kept hold of yours for the longest time. I had to go inside the house to Mama, but you told him to wait and you'd be out again in a moment. Later, when you came to say good night, you said, 'He's going off to war,' and I didn't know what war was. I couldn't go to sleep then because I was afraid you'd go off to war too. It was so very long ago. I am tired now. Will you come to see me another day?"

Gran came back with a young woman. "It's time for your rest, Miss Macready," she said.

I bent down and hugged her. "Good-bye, Miss Bessie."

She put a photo in my hand. "Take care of your soldier boy."

On the drive home, Gran says, "That was kind of you, Katie. I don't suppose Miss Macready has many visitors; she must have outlived most of her friends."

"It felt kind of strange, Gran. She thought I was someone she knew once and talked a bit about her childhood. Do you know she never liked that beautiful rocking horse? It scared her, gave her nightmares."

"I'll make a point of visiting her once in a while. Talk to her about the garden and the house."

The moment I turn off my bedside light this evening, Lillie appears. I've been half-expecting her. She stands by the dresser and stares at her reflection in the mirror. She experiments with hair styles, pinning her hair in a knot on top of her head, which makes her look older, finally letting it down loose on her shoulders. She checks her profile, smooths her dress, then sits on the foot of my bed. She curls her feet under her.

"His name is William, and his smile is nicer than ever. He waited for me." I'm not sure if she's talking to me or to herself.

"Didn't you know I would?" says a voice. A young man stands in front of her. He's in uniform. *Where did he*

come from? Is he really here? Is Lillie imagining him, or am I
dreaming them both?

When Lillie stands up, she is almost as tall as the
soldier. They hold hands, looking quietly at each other
for a long time. Their faces are filled with joy. I'm afraid
to speak, to switch on the light, to break the spell. The
soldier puts out his hand as if to touch a strand of her
hair, then sort of melts away into the shadows.

Lillie goes to the window. "We won't ever lose each
other again. He is the way I dreamed he would be. He'll
come back for me and we will be each other's family. A
family like they promised us."

"Lillie?" But she's gone before I get a chance to
speak to her.

HALIFAX, NOVA SCOTIA, CANADA

July 2005

Letters

I t's still early. Outside the seagulls scream their way to
the harbor. I sit bolt upright, instead of going back to
sleep the way I usually do. Something huge has happened, and for now I'm the only person in the whole
world who knows about it.

I don't know why it's taken me so long to work it out.
I should have guessed when Miss Macready confused me
with the girl who'd rescued her in Peterborough and
who became her nursemaid.

I jump out of bed and sit on the window seat, my
arms hugging my body in the early morning chill the
way I've watched Lillie's do. I pretend I'm her, looking
out at the rain before turning away to inspect the room
on the first day she arrived here. I know that this was her

room too. I've been sleeping in her bed, and she hung her dresses in the narrow wardrobe.

I'm almost the same age she was then, nearly fourteen. Miss Macready thought I was Lillie coming back to her. I bet Miss Bessie wasn't easy to manage, but she helped me discover that Lillie is my great-grandmother, the girl William fell in love with on board ship.

All those years they thought about each other, without knowing if they'd ever meet again. And then, on that day when they met in the park, Bessie knew she'd never have Lillie to herself again.

I feel as close to Lillie as I do to Angie – my best friend in Toronto – maybe closer. I think Lillie told me things she'd never told anyone else – how sad she was, how much she missed her mother, how cruel those women were to her. I get furious when I think of what happened. I wonder if she ever told William about that horrible Mr. Norman at the boarding house. I'm glad she trusted me enough to tell me. It would be awful to have to keep something like that locked up inside you.

I go over to the trunk and settle down on the floor of the alcove, the way Lillie always does. *The trunk! What if this is Lillie's trunk – the one she brought over to Canada, the one where she kept her things? What if the faint letter L on the lid is for her name and not Great-aunt Millicent's after all? If that's true, wouldn't Lillie hide her treasures in there to keep them safe?* Knowing Lillie, she'd make sure no one ever got the chance to trash her stuff again.

I open the lid, and start tossing out the spare quilts. I'm in a hurry, but then I stop. I'm behaving exactly the way Miss Alice did. I fold the quilts again tidily and hang them over the back of the cane chair.

"Lillie, I know you can hear me. Please don't mind me checking out your trunk. I think your ribbon might be there, and the picture from Helen that you told me about. I really want to look at them and hold them."

The trunk's empty now, except for some sheets of heavy brown wrapping paper on the bottom. I take them out, and all that's left is a little bunch of dried lavender and the faded striped canvas, lining the inside of the trunk. The stitches holding the canvas on the left side are coming loose. They look as if they'd come away once before and someone's repaired them with a different color. I can feel something lumpy under the cotton ticking. I pull at the threads until there's an opening wide enough to slide my hand inside.

I glance behind me, half-expecting to see Lillie looking over my shoulder.

My fingers touch a small package. There's just enough room for me to get hold of one corner and pull it out. I sit awhile, holding the parcel in my hands, turning it over, thinking about how long it's been hidden. I'm in no hurry, and to open it somehow seems like prying.

The name written across the front says LILLIE BRIDGES. My great-grandmother tied up this bundle of letters with cloth and a faded white ribbon. I run my finger along the length of the fabric. It's even older than Miss Bessie. *Did Lillie bring the ribbon with her from England? Is it the same one she wore for the Sunday school picnic, the one crumpled by Miss Alice?* Lillie must have washed it over and over to make it look like new again.

The present Lillie's mother gave her is here too. It's a picture postcard of a lady with glossy long hair, wearing a low-cut dress. The flower she's holding is a lily. The name printed on the front is LILLIE LANGTRY. A dried violet is glued to the back. *Once Helen gave me a picture and a flower. I'm going to keep them forever, Lillie said.*

The letters are signed by my great-grandfather William. I'm touching paper that Lillie and William touched. One by one I spread the letters out on the floor. It's hard to make out the words – some have faded, written in pencil instead of ink.

I imagine William writing his first letter to Lillie, his cap on the back of his head. I know just how his voice sounds because I heard him tell Lillie how he'd waited for her. *Didn't you know I would?* he'd said. I begin to read:

November 8, 1914, Salisbury, England

Dear Flower,

Or do you prefer me to call you Lillie? At last I know your name. I hope you don't think I'm being too forward, writing like this in my first letter to you, but after all, we have known each other since we were twelve years old. When I saw you that day in the Public Gardens with the little girl, I was afraid that she was yours — that you'd got married, before I realized you couldn't be old enough.

I never forgot you, Lillie. I always regretted not knowing who you are. Do you remember when you ran off to join the girls at the other end of the deck? I shouted out after you, "My name is William," but my voice got lost in the roar of the waves.

Once, thinking about you, when I was working at the furnace in the forge, I became careless and didn't turn my shirtsleeves under, as Mr. Armstrong had warned me to. Sparks caught in the folds of the fabric, and I've still got the scars. So I was reminded of you every day.

I'll write whenever I get the chance. The officers say we'll be sent over to the front as soon as we finish our training. I got lucky and am with the Second Canadian Division, the Cavalry Regiment, which is what I'd hoped for. I want to stay with the horses.

I've been given a weekend pass, so I'm off to London to meet my brother, Frankie. We haven't seen each other since I left for Canada. It will be great to catch up, after all this time. He writes that he can't wait to join the army next year, when he's eighteen.

Best wishes from your friend,
William Carr

November 16, 1914

My dear Lillie,
I'm back from my leave, the last for a while. Frankie met me at Paddington Station and the first thing we did, after we'd had a mug of tea at the refreshment stall, was to go looking for our old home. I'd forgotten how narrow and mean the streets were where we lived. Our house was a lot smaller than we'd both remembered. There wasn't a blade of grass, nor a tree in sight. No wonder Frankie's lungs were weak when he was a kid, breathing in that dusty damp air. He's fine now. He works as a market gardener outside London. I tell him he should emigrate after the war — come over here and find some good Canadian land to cultivate.

I can't bear reading this because I know that Frankie's going to die and will never have a chance to meet Lillie or to get that land. I'm almost afraid to read any more.

I'm homesick for Canada and for you, Lillie.
When I come back, we'll go on long walks and I'll
teach you to ride. If only we'd met sooner, before this
war started and separated us again. So much precious
time has been wasted.

Please send a photograph of yourself.
Your friend,
William

I go on browsing through and reading the letters
spread out on the floor.

January 2, 1915, France

My dear Lillie,

Your welcome parcel arrived in good time for Christmas
Day. I shared the delicious cake you baked with my
friends and I wear the muffler you knitted day and
night. Christmas Day was the strangest time. It really
was a day of peace, the way it should be. Men on both
sides of No Man's Land, the strip of ground that
divides us from the Germans, sang carols. We were
close enough to see the faces of the enemy. We called
out good wishes, and exchanged names and food.
Some showed photographs of their families. It was
good to forget about the war for a few hours. But what
I want to know is, how are we going to shoot each
other now? How do you kill a man with whom you

have shaken hands and who has told you his name?

I never want to spend another Christmas apart from
you.

Love,
William

The next letter is written on a page that looks like it's been torn out of an old exercise book. It's streaked with dirt, or maybe blood.

September 15, 1916, France

Darling Lillie,

We go forward a few yards, retreat, and advance over the same few yards of ground, over and over again. What's the use? I feel as if I've never lived anywhere else but a trench.

There's talk of a few days' leave soon. I can't wait for a bath and a change of clothes and a proper hot meal. No, there's no news of Frankie. He joined the Third London Rifles last year, but I haven't managed to meet up with him.

You asked me to tell you what the worst thing is out here. Well, apart from the lice and being so far away from you, it's the mud. I hate it. I'm used to Ontario mud. I'm used to axles and cattle and horses getting stuck and having to pull them out, but here it's a lot worse. It's like a stinking yellow bog. A man or a horse

*can disappear in seconds, and all that's left is a bubble
on the surface. A friend of mine went under yesterday.
He'd have had more of a chance going overboard cross-
ing the Atlantic.*

I'm sorry to write like this, Flower.

Your letters brighten even the gloomiest day.

Your loving
William

I find another sad note from Great-grandfather. It's
dated February 9, 1917. I can only manage to read a few
lines.

*The loss of so many beautiful horses breaks my heart.
This war is not for them. They should have been kept
out of it. The animals lie rotting on the battlefield, or
on the cobbled streets of what is left of the villages,
shelled by us or the enemy.*

October 3, 1917

*I'm so proud of you, Flower. I try to imagine you
working in a munitions factory, your beautiful hair
tucked under a kerchief. I'll bet you produce more shells
in a day than the rest of the girls put together. Tell the
supervisor you're spoken for, just so he knows.*

*Don't you worry about leaving young Bessie. A
big girl of ten doesn't need a nursemaid picking up after*

her. She'll be better off going to school in Quebec. You've spoiled her. Remember what we had to put up with in the orphanage?

Lillie, when the war is over (and now that you're helping the war effort, it won't last much longer), will you marry me? I will come back to you, and when I do, I'll never let you out of my sight again. I am, as always,

> *Your loving*
> *William*

There is one note from Lillie among the letters. It must have been written only a few days before the big explosion in Halifax harbor.

December 4, 1917, Halifax

Dearest Will,

Yes, I will marry you. I've been waiting for you to ask me. What took you so long? I made up my mind that day we met in the Gardens. I hope you don't think I'm too forward.

> *I love you,*
> *Lillie*

Suddenly I hear Lillie's laugh, see her face shining with happiness, the way it looked that night when she told me she'd found William again.

And then, William's last letter:

November 11, 1918

My own dear Flower,
The war is over at last. I'll be sailing home to you as
soon as I can.
> *Fondest love forever,*
> *William*

A sudden gust of wind scatters the pages all over the room. "You wanted me to find the letters, didn't you, Lillie? I am so happy that you and William got married."

I pick up the scattered pages and put them back in order, tie the ribbon round the package, and go down to breakfast.

Gran is making pancakes. "You are an early bird this morning! Sit down and keep your grandfather company." She slides two pancakes onto my plate, but I'm too excited to eat.

"Grandfather, I've got a present for you. Open it." I give him the package.

"It's not my birthday." He looks at Gran and then at me. He sees that I can't wait another second. "Right, I'll open it," he says.

He reads every word. When he's finished, he hands Gran the letters, pours himself a fresh mug of coffee, sits down beside me, and takes my hand. "Oh, Katie, thank you," he says.

My eyes well up because I can see how happy he is to have something from his parents. Gran's crying, the pancakes are burned, and nobody cares because in front of us is the history of our family.

Suddenly I remember the photo that Miss Bessie gave me, and rush upstairs to get it. Grandfather stares at Lillie's image. "I can't take it in – my mother here in our own garden," he says.

I have to repeat every single detail about Lillie saving Miss Bessie from the horses, and I try to explain why I thought of looking in the trunk . . . that it began with me seeing Lillie's shadow on the wall and how she talked to me through my dreams. Somehow I can't describe Lillie's visits: how she sang and cried, the way we talked and danced, and how we became friends.

The rain's stopped. The sun slants through the leaves of the apple tree. I'm almost sure I see Lillie standing behind the swing. She waves once, disappears, and I'm sad because I probably won't see her again.

I think I know why Great-grandfather didn't talk to his children about Lillie after she died – it was because he missed her so much. I miss her too.

Two days later, I fly home. Dad and Step had arrived the night before, so they're not too jet-lagged to hear about the letters.

They tell me about their trip. Dad says it was Step who found the book of photographs of the Yorkshire Moors for me. They're exactly what I need to help me picture where Mary Lennox lived when she arrived from India. The Moors are pretty much as I'd imagined from reading about them in *The Secret Garden* — cold, barren, and lonely in winter, but wild and romantic when heather and yellow gorse bushes bloom in spring and summer. . . .

For the first time ever, Dad, Stephanie, and I sit around the table talking like old friends. It's good to be home.

When I go upstairs to unpack, tucked deep down in the hidden pocket of my backpack is a small narrow box. I open it and find Lillie's white ribbon lying on a piece of black velvet.

There's a note:

> *Dear Katie,*
> *My mother would have wanted you to have her ribbon and I want you to have it too.*
> *Much love,*
> *Grandfather*

TORONTO, ONTARIO, CANADA

January, 2006

Hammy

I t is 1:00 A.M. on January 1. This is my first journal entry of the new year.

Last summer changed all of us, especially me. It sort of happened gradually, without us being aware of it, but we seem to be turning into a family.

The week I returned to school and the day before the auditions for the play, I looked at my book of photographs of the Moors — bleak and bare in winter, but covered with wildflowers in spring and summer. I tried to soak up the loneliness in the pictures . . . tried to remember what the wind sounded like on the night I heard Lillie crying . . . thought about how sad she was. That's the way Mary and Colin must feel.

Next morning, I tied Lillie's hair ribbon around my left wrist, the one with the freckle, as a lucky charm. I was totally nervous.

Our drama studio is in the school basement. No one seems to know what it was used for before it was converted into a theater space. Racks of costumes from previous productions line the walls. Boxes of props, steps, stools, ladders, freestanding lights, and a dimmer board provide just about any effects we need.

Mr. Keith encourages us to watch each other's auditions and listen to his comments. It's a fair way of running things, but scary too. After we'd finished our prepared speeches, Mr. Keith put us in two's and three's to read different scenes.

Next day some of us were called back. Mr. Keith said to help him make a final casting decision, he wanted us to tell him something about ourselves, and what we thought we could bring to the role we were auditioning for. He gave us a few minutes to prepare.

It was hard. I couldn't hide behind someone else's lines, the way I can when I'm just reading aloud. The words and thoughts had to come from inside me.

I understood what Mr. Keith was looking for, but I didn't know if I was brave enough to do it. I knew that if I wanted to play Mary Lennox, I'd have to fight to play her, and I could only do that by showing I wasn't afraid to share myself.

When it was my turn, I looked up at the studio wall, remembering the first time Lillie appeared to me. I wished I could see her shadow holding the flower. I sat down, and folded my hands in my lap, so that my fingers touched the ribbon she used to wear. (I had tied it around my wrist again — this time to give me courage.) I remembered the touch of Lillie's hands, how rough they'd felt from all the work she'd been made to do. I remembered how she never gave up hope, however awful her life was. I remembered how she spoke of things that must have been really painful to talk about. I won't let you down, Lillie. I promise.

I took a couple of deep breaths and began to speak: "I was seven when my mother died. When Mary wakes up in that big empty house in India, I think I know how lonely and scared she felt. I think I know how angry I'd be at having to leave everything familiar to go to a strange country to live with people I'd never met, even if they were relatives. And when she gets there, she doesn't feel she's wanted and wonders if she'll ever be part of a family again. It takes Mary a long time to find out that people care about her, and that she has to meet them halfway."

I stopped for a minute, trying to find the right words, not knowing quite how to go on. I looked up, and there she was — Lillie, I mean. Little and thin, wearing a shapeless dress. She was skipping along, as though down an alley. The boots she had on looked too big for her skinny legs. She stopped, held out her skirt, and began to dance a funny little dance. In a moment she was gone.

This was the hardest part. My fingers tightened around my wrist, touching the smooth ribbon. It gave me the confidence to continue: "This summer I found out about trusting people. I discovered that my great-grandparents were Home children — shipped over to Canada from orphanages in England. William Carr and Lillie Bridges and the other children had been promised kind families to take them in, and happy lives. Only the promises weren't often kept.

"Neither Lillie nor William ever gave up hope for a better life, and it made them stronger. Then at last they found each other and became the family they'd both been hoping and waiting for.

"I think I can play Mary Lennox. I understand the pain of that kind of loneliness and how it can help you to grow."

There was a dead silence. Mr. Keith finally said, "Well done. Next please." I got up and walked back to my chair to listen to the others, feeling as tired as if I'd crossed the ocean myself.

Two days later, the cast notice for The Secret Garden was posted:

Mary Lennox — Kaitlin Carr

★

*Dad and Step and I kind of decided together on names
for the baby. It was a pretty obvious choice after the dis-
covery of the letters: William Hamish if it was a boy and
Lillie Helen if a girl. Helen was my suggestion, and
Step really liked the name. Somehow, when we talked
about the baby, it was such a mouthful saying both
names. We got into the habit of shortening it to Hammy.
Hopefully it won't stick, or the poor kid will go through
life being called something that sounds like a hamster.*

*Step thinks babies can understand stuff even before
they're born, and kept telling Hammy she did not want
him to appear early, and to hold his arrival until after
December 10th, the final night of* The Secret Garden.

*Mr. Keith had asked Step to coordinate costumes,
and she ended up making a lot of them, so naturally
she was invited to the Saturday night cast and crew
party. Dad dropped us both off at Mr. Keith's house,
and said he'd be back after he'd checked out some
embryos in the lab.*

I was talking to the guy who played Colin in The
Secret Garden *when Angie grabbed me and said
Stephanie was asking for me. I found her on the stairs,
clinging to the banisters. Mel had already phoned for
an ambulance and Mr. Keith was on the cell to my
dad. The "drama club baby" was on its way.*

*When the ambulance finally got there, Step tried
being noble and didn't want me to miss the party. But,*

as I tactfully pointed out, Dad would kill me if I stayed behind. Actually, I wanted to go with her.

Lillie Helen Carr made her appearance at 12:05 P.M. on December 11, six days before my fourteenth birthday. She does not resemble a hamster. We think she's perfect! She has Dad's chin, Step's eyes, and a few stray white blonde hairs.

I close my journal and lie awake looking at Mom's portrait. How differently I feel about everything now! My sister is three weeks old today and, so far, has not grasped that there is a difference between day and night. In other words, she sleeps and we don't. Dad mutters pathetically about sleep deprivation, and I tell him he's getting old.

Last week I had to stop him boasting to Step, for the twentieth time, how I slept through the night at two weeks. "No way. Memory loss, Dad," I said. Then I suddenly had a brilliant idea. "How about me baby-sitting one night a month so you two can go out to dinner by yourselves, like normal people?" Dad said, "I'd never keep awake long enough to eat!" Step said, "You're an angel, Katie, and I'll do the same for you one day." They've booked me for next Friday night, and Mel and Angie are coming over for pizza.

My grandparents phoned just before New Year's. Gran offered me a paying job next summer. They've got a waiting list of guests already. I'm to serve breakfasts, help clean up, and make beds. It will mean getting up at dawn, like Lillie did. But I'll get afternoons and evenings off. Gran's going to make my gingerbread the house specialty.

I'll be paid fifty dollars a week and tips. Step suggested they fly out to join me at the end of the summer. "We could drive to PEI. Katie and I want to see *Anne of Green Gables*. Rumor has it that it's next year's Christmas play. You could watch the baby for a couple of hours, darling, couldn't you?" she said to Dad.

"Fly? Are you serious? Will Hammy, I mean Lillie, be on a routine by then?" Dad said.

"I've no idea," Step replied.

"Awesome. Thanks, Step," I said.

"I guess I'm outnumbered. Fine, it's settled," Dad said, but he didn't seem to mind being outnumbered one bit.

Routine has become a dirty word in this house. Step's awful mother paid a flying visit yesterday, just before lunch. She was drenched in perfume, which is really selfish because she's been told it gives me allergies. Hammy sneezed, so she's probably allergic too.

The conversation went along the following lines (to Step): "You look exhausted, poor darling, and so washed out. Why don't you run upstairs and put a face on and I'll hold the baby?" She grabbed Hammy, who had the good sense to start yelling. Step took the baby into the kitchen to feed her. Her mother followed and went on and on about routines. "Do you mean to say, you feed her whenever she wants? Babies need to be put on a strict four-hour schedule. That's how you and Giles were raised. Is little Lillie sleeping through the night yet?"

Step said, "Are you staying for lunch, Mother? We're having leftovers, dolmades and Greek salad."

"You know perfectly well, Stephanie, Greek food gives me indigestion. I just popped in to wish you Happy New Year." She cooed loudly at Hammy, who showed perfect timing by starting to wail again. "And don't worry about Lillie's hair, dear. Some babies are bald for months. I'm sure she will be very pretty. It's too bad she doesn't resemble anyone in our family. Giles was a truly beautiful child."

I'd had enough, and no warning looks from Step were going to shut me up. "Most people think Lillie looks like my dad, and they seem to agree he's pretty good-looking for his age."

Her mother turned to Step, who was trying to keep a straight face and not having much success. "I can see you have your hands full. I'll call you tomorrow, dear."

When Dad came home a few minutes later, Step and I were almost hysterical and Hammy was screaming. He took the babe from Step, and said, "You are all giddy from lack of sleep."

Step said, "Katie and I were just discussing how good-looking you are for your age." And that started us off again. After we'd calmed down, Step took Hammy up for her nap, and Dad and I made lunch.

I told Dad I didn't think Step's mother was very supportive. Is she jealous, maybe? He said, "You've noticed." Then he said something that is pretty nice to hear: "If Lillie Helen Carr turns out even half as well as her big sister, I'll consider myself a lucky old man."

It's past 2 A.M. Hammy is making little mewling noises. She likes company and hasn't got used to sleeping in her own room yet, away from Dad and Step. The hall light is on and I creep into the nursery, pick her up, and talk to her. She works hard at her smile, but it's not quite there yet. I show her how the night-light casts a sprinkling of stars on the wall above her crib.

Suddenly Lillie's shadow appears, standing among the stars, the way I saw her that first time last summer. "Look, Hammy, that's your great-grandmother Lillie coming to take a look at you. You were named for her. This is the song she used to sing: Ta-ra-ra Boom-de-ay, Ta-ra-ra Boom-de-ay."

I wait until my sister's eyes begin to close and then I tuck her back in her crib. "Happy New Year," I whisper to both of them.

The End

Afterword

Of the more than 100,000 homeless children sent to Canada from Britain between 1867 and 1967, 30,000 came from Dr. Barnardo's Homes.